CW01513292

Fractured Echoes

You can't fight what you can't remember.

J J Noad

First published in Great Britain in 2025.

Copyright © J J Noad, 2025. All rights reserved.
All rights reserved. No part of this publication may be
reproduced, stored, or transmitted in any form or by any means,
electronic, mechanical, photocopying, recording, scanning, or
otherwise, without written permission from the publisher. It is illegal
to copy this book, post it to a website, or distribute it by any other
means without permission.

The right of J J Noad to be identified as the author of this work
has been asserted by them in accordance with the Copyright, Design
and Patents Act 1988.
ISBN: 9798291087978

Disclaimer:
This is a work of fiction. Names, characters, businesses, places,
events, and incidents are either the product of the author's
imagination or used fictitiously. Any resemblance to actual persons,
living or dead, or actual events is purely coincidental.

Dedication

For Helen, Elliott, and Megan
For your patience, good humour, and ability to ignore the fact I
talked to myself for a year.
Thanks for not changing the locks.
This was written with love and possibly too many biscuits.

Chapter 1

Off-season Blackpool blinked with the last breath of neon. The promenade stretched under a flat, metallic sky, its old promises of spectacle dulled to silence. Shutters clattered faintly in the wind, the scent of fryer grease and saltwater hung in the air, spoiled and clinging. The lights, when they worked, blinked erratically. Gulls drifted overhead without conviction, their cries thin, aimless. The town wasn't asleep. It was vacant. Left behind after the show closed, the seats still warm, the stage bare.

Inside The Seagull's Rest, the air was thick with familiar decay. Fryer oil had seeped into the walls long before the smoking ban. Wood darkened with age and damp creaked underfoot. A television buzzed faintly above the bar, showing some quiz show from a year no one bothered to remember.

Mick Holden sat in his corner, hunched over a half-pint, one hand resting on the curved lip of the glass, the other sunk deep in his coat pocket. He sat as if the seat remembered him. His clothes had stiff creases from old folds; his belly rested heavily on his belt. Fifty-eight, grey where hair still clung, possessing the kind of heaviness that didn't fight back anymore. His life had become a slow, habitual drift through the same few streets, the same few voices. Everything blurred into routine, the edges worn like carpet under old habits.

The quiz show flickered, the sound slightly off. A woman, middle-aged, hollow-eyed, hesitated at the buzzer. The host smiled tightly.

"What is the capital of Norway?"

Mick muttered, "Oslo," without thinking.

He used to shout answers at the telly once. Harry would roll his eyes, pretending not to care, but he'd stay until the end of the show anyway. Mick hadn't realised how much that mattered. Not until the silence afterwards started feeling bigger than the room.

A second later, the woman said it aloud in almost exactly the same tone. He frowned, not startled but faintly unsettled, like something was where it shouldn't be. There was something disconcerting about it, something primal. Not fear, exactly. More like stepping onto a stair you thought was there and finding nothing under your foot. A wrongness that wasn't content to be ignored. Another question came. Again, his lips moved before hers. Then another, and another, always a breath ahead. The phrasing, the hesitation; it wasn't just knowing the answer, it was knowing the rhythm of her thought. By the fourth question, he wasn't watching anymore. His stomach had gone cold and heavy. He knew the ending before the host spoke. The woman would falter at the final question. The audience would sigh. The host would soften his voice. Then, an advert for biscuits, an old brand, the kind you never saw anymore.

And it played out exactly that way.

He turned toward the bar mirror, though he didn't know why. His face stared back at him, distorted slightly by streaks of old polish and the yellow tint of nicotine. Behind the reflection, nothing stirred. But something crawled at the edge of his thoughts, just beyond recall. Not fear, an older instinct. Like remembering you'd left the gas on.

The fruit machine pinged. Sharp, artificial. A woman stooped near the bar. Keys clattered to the carpet and bounced once. She bent, swore softly, scooped them up in one motion, her head tilting as she stood.

Mick's hand tensed around his glass. He'd seen it before.

Not like déjà vu. Not almost. An exact repeat. The same motion, the same muttered curse, the slight shake of her head. A memory from sleep. He had dreamt this. Last night.

He took a measured sip of beer. The glass trembled slightly in his grip. Maybe coincidence. That word again, déjà vu. But it didn't settle. Something pressed at the edge of thought, faint but insistent.

The door opened, and cold air rolled in. A couple stepped through, wind-beaten, dressed for the sea. They didn't look at him, didn't even pause. They went straight to the table near the back. Then the fruit machine dinged again. This time, the sound hung in the air just a second too long. He turned his head slowly. A woman bent to the floor. Keys. His stomach clenched. The motion, the angle of her body, the timing, it wasn't like the dream. It was the dream. Again.

He wiped his mouth and stared down at his pint. The pub felt distant now, as if he was behind glass. Sound softened. Glasses clinked in the background, a burst of laughter rose and fell, but it all seemed detached, muffled. The door opened again. Mick looked this time. The man who entered wore a long dark coat, heavy with rain. He moved without hurry, eyes scanning the room, not searching for a table, not looking for anyone in particular. It was the look of someone making a quiet inventory.

At the bar, Sheila stood with one hand on the towel. He said something low. She nodded and poured a measure. No chat, no warmth, just quick movements, and silence. He didn't drink. He didn't sit. He waited, perfectly still. Then his eyes shifted. They found Mick. Not a glance. Not coincidence. The stare was fixed as if he'd always known where to find him.

Mick's hand drifted from the glass. He held the man's gaze, but the cold in his stomach deepened. He knew this man. From the dream. From last night. From somewhere he couldn't place. And now, finally, the man saw him too.

Chapter 2

Mick woke with a stale taste in his mouth, dry and sour at the edges. His head throbbed with that slow, rhythmical ache that didn't ask for paracetamol, just silence and time. It wasn't quite a hangover. He'd had those, knew their shape, but this was something duller, stranger, a pressure behind the eyes, not from drink but from something half-buried, just out of reach. It lingered, stubborn and nameless.

Light leaked through the sun-faded curtains, thin and colourless, spreading across the peeling wallpaper in weak, directionless streaks. It lit nothing. Revealed nothing. The flat was still, close with the smell of sleep and sweat and something faintly metallic, coppery, like the inside of a coin jar. Mick lay without moving, letting the ceiling come into focus, waiting for his thoughts to align themselves into something manageable. But even as he tried, last night began to take shape, not as memory, but as something deeper.

The quiz show played out again behind his eyelids. The answers he'd spoken before the questions were fully formed. The woman at the fruit machine, keys scattering across the carpet, the same turn of her head, the same words mouthed under her breath. And the man in the coat. The way he had appeared and not departed. There'd been no goodbye, no motion toward the door. One moment present, the next gone. No sound, no shift. As if time had blinked. Mick didn't remember looking away, yet the man had vanished just the same, leaving behind nothing but the certainty that he had been there.

He rose slowly, the weight in his limbs matched only by the one pressing behind his ribs. The kitchen was colder than the rest of the flat, and the tile floor was unforgiving underfoot. He filled the kettle and stared out the window as the water began to boil. The sea between rooftops had no colour to speak of. It sat flat, indifferent. As the kettle clicked off, he poured the coffee and stood by the window, watching the waves move without energy, rising and sinking without purpose. He burned his tongue on the first sip but barely registered it. The heat grounded him, but only just.

He wanted to believe he'd imagined it all, that his brain had stitched together old memories and half-forgotten dreams. He could have seen that episode before. Could have overheard someone drop their keys once and remembered it the wrong way round. He told himself these things not to be convinced, but to slow the churn inside him. He needed structure, motion, something routine. The streets, a newspaper, breakfast somewhere that didn't smell like his own sheets.

But as he stepped out into the street, the strangeness followed. The buildings were all where they should be, the chipped kerbstones and boarded-up amusements unchanged. But the air had shifted, still thick with salt and fryer grease but now threaded with something acrid, faint but persistent. Like burnt plastic. Like something recently extinguished.

He walked slower than usual, hands buried in his coat pockets, eyes flicking across the familiar. Shopfronts, café windows, the sluggish silhouette of the Tower in the distance, but there was a film over everything, a strange flatness to the light, as though it belonged somewhere else. When he pushed open the door to the newsagent's, the little bell gave its usual jangle, though it sounded oddly flat. The air inside was warm, filled with paper, dust, and polish. He nodded to the man behind the counter, reached for a paper, then paused.

The date was right. But the headline, something about it, was off. Not dramatic or strange in itself, but not quite close to normal. As if something had shifted a fraction. He stared at it for a few seconds longer than he meant to, trying to remember what he'd expected to see instead, but nothing surfaced. Just the sure, crawling certainty that the page in front of him shouldn't exist.

"You alright, mate?" the shopkeeper asked, tilting his head.

Mick blinked and nodded. "Thought I read something else online earlier," he said, voice thick.

"Yeah, well. They're always changing things, aren't they?" came the reply, already distracted.

Outside again, Mick flipped through the paper, scanning headlines with no real focus. It all felt thinner than it should. A version of the day without its weight. The story on page five was familiar, though he couldn't say how or why. He tucked the paper under his arm and kept walking, trying to shake the sense that the day was repeating in ways he couldn't quite prove.

When he arrived at The Seagull's Rest around noon, the pub was nearly empty, holding that mid-morning lull before the regulars drifted in. The fruit machine blinked lazily in the corner. Behind the bar, Sheila was drying glasses, slow and methodical, her eyes fixed on the task rather than the door.

"I thought you said you weren't coming in today," she said as he stepped in.

Mick frowned. "I didn't say that."

"You did. Last night. Said you had something to do."

He opened his mouth, closed it again. He didn't remember that. Not even vaguely. "Must've changed my mind," he muttered, sliding onto the stool that knew his shape.

She didn't press the point. Just poured him a pint and went back to her glasses. He drank without tasting, his thoughts already elsewhere. The newspaper. Her comment. Another detail that didn't sit right. Not loud, but sharp enough to feel. And then he saw the man.

Same table. Same posture. As if last night had never ended. It was as if the man had been sitting there all along, waiting for Mick to finally notice him again. There was no surprise in the man's expression. No recognition, either. Just stillness.

Mick turned back to his pint, the warmth draining from his hands. He set the glass down, pushed himself upright. "Gotta go," he said without looking at Sheila. She didn't answer, or maybe she hadn't heard.

The air outside was colder than before. Or he had become more sensitive to it. He stood still on the pavement, trying to collect himself, the pub door clicking shut behind him. He needed to think. Needed something to make sense. Then he heard it.

A voice, level and close. "You've noticed it, haven't you?"

Mick turned. The man in the coat stood there, just feet away, eyes calm, face unreadable.

"Noticed what?" Mick asked, more breath than voice.

"That things aren't the way they should be." There was no menace in the tone. No warmth either. Just quiet certainty. The man's eyes didn't shift. His expression didn't change. Mick stared at him, every instinct urging him to move, but he couldn't.

"Don't worry," the man said, with something that might have been a smile, though it passed so quickly it was hard to say. "You're not the first."

Then he turned and walked away, not hurried, not slow. Just certain. As if the conversation had ended the moment he'd spoken. Mick stayed where he was, hands twitching at his sides, his throat too dry to swallow. *Not the first.* The words repeated in his head, slow and heavy. Not the first.

Chapter 3

The Seagull's Rest was busier than usual that evening. The low murmur of conversation moved like smoke between tables, occasionally broken by a laugh too sharp, splintering the air. Glasses clinked, chairs scraped across the worn floor, and in the corner, the fruit machine blinked its synthetic colours, mostly ignored except by a woman feeding it coins with a detached rhythm, her gaze fixed far beyond the screen.

Mick stepped inside and let the warmth close in, the scent of old beer settling over him, thick and familiar. Outside, the promenade had been damp, the air restless with the tang of brine and wet concrete, that unmistakable Blackpool rot when the tide lingered too long. He'd walked for hours, trying to outpace the sense of wrongness that had settled just beneath his ribs, but it had followed, patient and tightening. Even now, seated, it remained. An echo of the stranger's words from the night before lodged deep in his spine. "You're not the first." Simple. Flat. Spoken like a fact.

The pub looked the same, but Mick wasn't certain it was. Or maybe he no longer trusted his ability to tell. Gary sat at his usual table, one arm resting on the sticky varnish of the table, pint halfway gone. His clothes sat between tidy and tired, creased in a way that suggested care long abandoned. He stared at nothing. It might have been boredom. It might have been peace. Hard to tell which.

Mick slid into the booth opposite. "Alright, Gary?"

Gary looked up slowly, squinting like Mick had arrived too soon. "Christ," he muttered. "You look like shite."

Mick gave a dry exhale and rubbed at his face. "Yeah. Cheers."

Gary chuckled, a low, rattled sound. "Another day of deep thought and philosophical torment, was it?"

There was a pause. Mick didn't answer. He thought about telling Gary. About the birthdays he'd missed, the calls that got shorter until they stopped altogether. About Harry. But Gary wasn't the type to lean in. And Mick wasn't the type to ask for company anymore. Some part of him kept watching the room. The man in the coat wasn't there, but that absence did little to settle him. It felt worse. Something gone quiet that shouldn't be.

Sheila appeared, one hand on her hip. "You having one, Mick?"

He nodded. "Yeah, cheers."

For a moment, her expression faltered. A flicker. Something behind the eyes. It passed quickly, but not before he felt it. Then she turned back to the bar. The spell broke. Mick glanced at Gary, who watched with vague amusement, sensing drama but not yet invested.

"What's up with you?" Gary asked.

Mick considered brushing it off. But the pressure behind his eyes wouldn't ease. "Weird couple of days."

Gary grinned faintly. "Everything's weird if you think about it too much."

Maybe. Maybe it was all tricks of light and memory. But just as Mick opened his mouth to steer them elsewhere, something shifted. A voice rose from the bar, then another. Fragmented at first, then clear.

"Yeah, that old hotel down the promenade. Shutting down, finally."

Mick froze.

A laugh followed. "About bloody time. Place has been falling apart for years."

His hand tightened on the table. He'd heard that before. Not as gossip. Not in passing. In a dream. Last night. Word for word. Same voices. Same rhythm. A perfect replication.

Gary was still talking. Mick couldn't follow. His ears filled with blood, each heartbeat suddenly audible. The voices at the bar carried on, cheerful, unaware. Like the woman who dropped her keys. Like the quiz show. A sequence repeating.

Gary's voice cut through. "Oi. Mick. You listening?"

Mick turned his head slowly. "That conversation. Did you hear it?"

Gary gave a wary look. "What about it?"

"I dreamed it. Last night."

Pause. Then a snort. "Jesus, Mick. You need a hobby."

"I'm serious."

Gary smirked, sipped his pint. "Déjà vu, mate. Everyone gets it."

But it wasn't that. Déjà vu was vague. This was exact. Like the world had already run through the scene and decided to show it again. Déjà vu didn't usually leave your mouth dry, your hands cold. Didn't usually peel something loose inside you, a layer you hadn't realised was stitched so thin. He stared into his pint, unsure whether to say more.

"You ever had a dream so real it happened the next day?"

Gary sighed. "I dream about all sorts. Doesn't make me a bloody prophet."

Maybe Mick should've kept it to himself. He drained half his pint, bitterness washing down his frustration. Around them, the pub carried on. But a new idea crept in. What if it wasn't just overheard lines or flickering quiz shows?

That night, sleep was slow to come. The wind scraped at the windows. Mick lay tangled in damp sheets, his thoughts circling. Images surfaced, then sank. And then, without warning, the dream returned.

He was back in The Seagull's Rest. Same low lights, same voices, same smell thick in the wood. But something was wrong. Smoke slid along the ceiling beams, faint at first, then thicker. It oozed from cracks in the walls, curled around picture frames. The air shimmered. A roar built behind the bar, muffled, rising. Fire bloomed. Sudden. Violent. It climbed the panelling, painted the walls orange and black. Bottles burst. The heat pressed inward. Suffocating. No one moved. The pub was empty now. Still burning. Silence settled, dense.

He woke gasping, chest slick with sweat, sheets twisted around his legs, clinging. He sat up, rubbed his face. Just a dream, he told himself. But it echoed through his limbs. Not a warning. Something worse. A glimpse of what had already been decided.

The next evening, he told himself to stay in. He boiled an egg. Let it go cold. Switched on the telly. Switched it off. Still, his feet found their path back to The Seagull's Rest. As he stepped inside, his eyes swept the room before the warmth reached him. No fire. No smoke. Just the pub.

He breathed out slowly. Maybe it had only been a bad dream folded too tightly around a bad mood. But then the door creaked open behind him. Not fast. Not loud. Just that slow, deliberate motion the body registers before the mind does. He felt it. Like a drop in temperature. As if the world paused to inhale.

He turned. The man in the coat stepped inside. Moved like someone who already knew the room. And as he made his way to the table at the back, the same table, Mick felt something worse than fear. The distinct certainty that he hadn't just arrived. He'd been there all along.

Chapter 4

The kettle screamed. Mick let it wail a second too long before yanking it off the hob. The sound sliced through the silence of the flat and died in a single, breathless wheeze. He poured the boiling water into a chipped mug, not looking, the steam rising in pale, uncertain lines. He stirred the instant coffee with the handle of the spoon, as he always did when no one was there to see. The motion was slow, deliberate. Something about it obeyed him. In a world beginning to tilt, that stir was his.

The notebook sat open on the table, as if it had never been gone. He'd found it the night before, tucked behind takeaway menus and receipts from places long gone, next to a letter addressed to someone he no longer remembered being. The pages were yellowed, the cover worn down to softness. It might've once been meant for shopping lists. He had never used it, not until now. Yet the blank lines had drawn him in, quiet and insistent.

He sat, biro in hand. The coffee cooled beside him, untouched. The flat's silence had weight, pressing into his ears. He hesitated. Then, with care, he wrote: *Dream: The Blackpool tram breaks down outside The Seagull's Rest. A woman in a red coat swears and checks her watch.* The words looked harmless, almost dull. But his grip had tightened around the pen. It was a test. If it happened just as he'd dreamed, he'd know. He refused to think beyond that.

He slid the notebook back into the drawer, closed it without drama. Told no one. Not Gary. Not Sheila. Not even himself, not out loud.

He moved through the day in the usual way, shopping at odd hours, walking streets half-empty, nodding at faces that didn't quite register. But the dream stayed behind his eyes.

At 5:37, with the sky the colour of old ash, he was halfway down the promenade. Hands in coat pockets. Then he saw it.

The tram had stopped in the middle of the road. The driver hunched over the radio, frowning. A sluggish trail of traffic gathered behind it. Inside, passengers stood without movement, their faces dim behind the glass. Then, a woman in a red coat stepped down, her heels clicking on the pavement. She shook her head, checked her watch, muttered something low.

The cadence struck him. Mick froze. He didn't blink.

The world went on. Cars edged forward. A gull shrieked. Somewhere, a door slammed. The air carried the faint, scorched tang of something burnt and forgotten. But none of it touched him. The moment didn't need confirmation. It simply was.

He turned and entered The Seagull's Rest. The warmth hit him. Sheila looked up from the glasses. "You alright?" she asked, neutral but edged.

He waited too long. "Knackered," he said. She nodded and pulled a pint.

Gary was already at the usual table, grumbling over a newspaper that looked three days old. Mick sat without speaking, listening to the pub's sounds: voices, glass clinks, the dull chirp of the fruit machine. It was like hearing the room from behind a closed window, everything faint, everything far away. The pint stayed untouched. Only his pulse was real, steady, and slow. This was happening. And it wasn't stopping.

That night, the dream returned. A man stepped from the kerb, takeaway coffee in hand. The cup slipped, spilled down his leg. A blue car idled outside the pub. A cat darted across the tram tracks. Brakes squealed. Mick woke with a jolt, sweat cooling on his back. The air thick, unmoving. It hadn't felt like a dream. It had been shown to him.

He reached for the notebook in the dark, hands trembling. He wrote: *Man spills coffee. Blue car outside the pub. Cat crosses tram tracks.*

The words came easily, like they were waiting. Not a choice. A duty. He didn't analyse. He wrote because he had to.

The day moved around him again, a loop rethreaded. And just like before, it unfolded. The same man, the stumble, the brown shoes soaked with coffee. The same car. The same cat. Mick watched, frozen. This wasn't repetition. It was arrangement.

But then it shifted. That night's dream altered. The man caught the cup. It wobbled but held. The car, now red. The cat never appeared. Mick woke, gasping, lungs tight, the air suddenly wrong. Not fear. Realisation.

At the table, coffee cooling untouched beside him, he noticed the notebook already open. The handwriting precise, unfamiliar. He traced the ink's curve. It felt like a message left for someone else. He turned back a page, then another. The dreams weren't repeating. They were changing. The future wasn't fixed. It was being redrafted.

His breath caught. What did that mean for the fire? If these visions bent and shifted, was the fire not inevitable but suggestible? Was he witnessing, or was he shaping? His hand tightened on the pen, knuckles pale. The future was shifting. And he wasn't just watching anymore.

Chapter 5

The cold had worked its way in by the time Mick reached the Chronicle. Not the kind of cold you shrug off. It was in the joints, at the base of the neck, the places where aches learn to settle and keep quiet. He stood a moment, coat tight, looking up at the building. The brickwork was the same dull red, now darkened by rain, the windows filmed with a kind of resignation. Another door he'd hesitated at once, a lifetime ago. A birthday party he'd been too proud to crash, even though the invitation had been written in the curve of a six-year-old's hand. Harry had waited then. He doubted anyone would wait now.

He shifted his weight. The place hadn't changed. Still irrelevant. Like the letters he'd once written and never sent. The conversations rehearsed and never spoken. Some things didn't change because you never gave them the chance. Once, the Chronicle had printed stories that mattered. You could smell the ink on your fingers and know it meant something. Now, it was council noise, limp features, and crime pieces flattened into summaries.

Somewhere behind those glass panes was Alice Whittaker.

She had been the sort who stayed after the lights went off. Fights with editors. Phone calls that went on too long. She'd written stories that made people wince, flinch, react. But that had been years ago. He didn't know if she'd remember him. He didn't know if she'd care. But he was running out of people to trust.

Inside, the reception sat in late-afternoon light. Fluorescents buzzed overhead, low, and constant. The woman at the desk didn't look up from her screen.

"Can I help you?"

He hesitated. "I'm looking for Alice Whittaker."

She blinked once, gaze flicking toward the clock behind him. "She's in. What's it about?"

He didn't answer straight away. "Something she might want to see."

The woman gave a neutral shrug and nodded toward the main room. "Third desk from the left."

He saw her before he got there. Some people blur over time. Alice hadn't. Her posture was the same, straight-backed, present. Her fingers moved quick over the keys. She looked up.

"Mick Holden," she said, the name landing slow. "Well. That's a face."

He scratched his jaw. "Been busy."

"If you're here to reminisce, buy me a drink later. I've got a deadline."

He reached into his coat, pulled out a clipping, and placed it on the desk. "Tell me what you see."

She glanced down, skimmed. An old piece, guesthouse fire, south promenade, one of those filler stories for slow news days. "And?"

He laid a second clipping beside it.

Same fire. Same headline. But different. She looked from one to the other. Slower now. Her eyes narrowed. Different photo. A quote gone. Dates that didn't quite match. Small shifts. Enough to notice if you knew where to look.

"Where'd you get these?"

"I cut them out last year. Same day, same paper."

She didn't speak. The lines between her brows deepened. She reached for her screen, typed. The Chronicle's archive came up blank. She tried another search. Narrowed it. Broadened. Nothing. The system gave her a polite silence in return. She leaned forward, eyes hard, fingers tighter on the mouse. Another search. External database. Still nothing. Not even a mention.

"It's not here," she said without looking up. "They've erased it."

He nodded. "Thought so."

She didn't ask what he meant. She already knew.

Alice turned back to her screen, moving faster now. She searched her bylines. Cross-referenced. 'Alice Whittaker fire investigation.' The screen gave her a full second before flashing up: No results. She sat still, longer than she should have. When she finally spoke, her voice had thinned.

"I wrote that story. Five years ago. Gas leak at a B&B. I remember it." Her voice sharpened. "I remember it."

"Me too," Mick said.

She closed the tabs. The cursor blinked in an empty field. She pulled out her notebook. Flipped through.

The dates were wrong. Her writing slanted differently. Names were crossed out. Notes rewritten. Something in the ink had shifted.

Then she stopped. One name.

"Alan Cleary," she murmured. "Went missing ten years ago. Worked arcade security. Quiet. Nobody noticed he was gone, not at first."

"No trace?" Mick asked.

"Nothing."

She flipped again, found a line at the edge of the page. Read it aloud.

"I think reality is changing. I don't think I was supposed to notice."

The words hung between them. Mick didn't speak. He didn't need to. Because now she was noticing, too.

Chapter 6

The town smelled of salt and rot. Not the sharp tang of sea air, but the slow decay that rose from between the paving stones and settled into the walls. Mick walked with his hands buried deep in his coat pockets, head lowered against the damp breeze. It had rained earlier. He could feel it in the slickness beneath his boots, the way puddles formed in the cracked asphalt. The wind carried weight, not just cold, but something heavier. A damp that worked into the bones.

At the top of the narrow path, he slowed. The street ahead was quiet. Not just end-of-day quiet, but something thinner, as if the life had been pressed out of it. He turned the corner. Gary's house.

He stopped. The door was boarded up. Not locked. Sealed. Thick wooden planks nailed without care across the frame, across the windows, too. It wasn't preservation. It was erasure. The nails stuck out. The timber was fresh.

Mick stared, something tight coiling in his chest. The house hadn't been abandoned. It had been removed. Not just wiped away in anger or haste. Sealed up like a mistake the town didn't want to admit it had made. As if someone had a blueprint for forgetting. Not a part of the street anymore. He stepped forward and knocked twice. The sound died on the wood. No echo. No reply.

He pulled out his phone, fingers stiff, and dialled. One ring. "The number you have dialled is not recognised." He frowned, tried again. Same message. The tone of it final. As if the number had never been his to call. The wind picked up, shifting the leaves, setting a drainpipe clattering.

He stood another moment, staring at the door, then turned, walking faster now, boots loud in the emptiness.

The Seagull's Rest was open. Its light pooled across the pavement, warm and familiar. The air that met him was thick with old beer and something sourer, less easy to name, as he pushed the door. Inside: voices, darts, glass against wood. Just as it had always been.

He shook off the damp and scanned the room, eyes drawn to the back tables.

Someone was there. Not Gary. A stranger. Leaning back, pint in hand, talking to Sheila like he belonged. Mick's stomach shifted. Something steady gave way.

He crossed to the bar.

"Sheila."

She was wiping a glass. Casual. "Alright, Mick?"

"Where's Gary?"

She looked up, puzzled. "Who?"

He gripped the edge of the bar. "Gary. My mate. Always at that table."

She followed his gaze. A faint frown. "Mick... no one's sat there regular in years."

He turned. A few heads looked up, then down again. The conversation dimmed, just a notch. The room wasn't different, not to look at. But something had gone soft underneath.

"You know him. Grey hair. Talks about the old days. Pint of bitter."

One of the other regulars, Kev, gave a nervous laugh. "Think you're winding us up, mate."

Mick didn't reply. No pint glass. No coat. Nothing. The spot wasn't Gary's anymore. Had it ever been?

"He was here last night," he said. "You served him."

She didn't argue. Just softened, like someone faced with grief or confusion. "Mick, love... maybe you're thinking of someone else."

He left before she could say more.

The walk home stretched. The streets shone wet under the lamps, but even their reflections looked altered now.

The rhythm of the town had gone strange. It pressed in, quiet but tense. The smell of salt clung closer, mixed with something chemical. The air felt faintly scorched.

In the flat, the air was thick. The scent of beer clung to the carpet and fabric. He didn't take off his coat. Turned on the lamp. Blinked at the light. Started moving. Drawers. Newspapers. Picture frames. Cushions. Boxes untouched in years. He didn't know what he was looking for, only that something had to be there. A trace.

At the back of an old folder, he stopped. A photo. Ten years ago. The Seagull's Rest. A group of them, arms slung over shoulders, pints raised. Curtain behind them. Dartboard. That crooked frame. He was there, in the middle. Younger. Sheila, beside him, caught in laughter. And on his other side… Gary. His thumb traced the shoulder. The glass in Gary's hand. The crease of his coat. But the face wasn't there. Not blurred. Not obscured. Just missing. A blank where something should have been.

He sat on the edge of the bed. The photo limp in his fingers. The silence settled close. In the kitchen, the kettle clicked off. He didn't move. The lamp hummed faintly. The air, wrong. Not haunted. Altered. As though something had passed through, almost carefully.

Then came the sound. The letterbox rattled once. No knock. No footstep. Just the metal flap swinging and falling back. He didn't get up. He didn't need to.

He sat there, the photo in his lap, eyes fixed on the space where Gary's face should have been. The quiet deepened, broken now and then by the faint creak of metal. He listened, not expecting anything, but because something was still nearby. The room hadn't finished settling. And behind the door, something waited.

Chapter 7

Mick sat at Alice's desk, his notebook open between them, full of things neither of them read aloud. The pages were crowded with notes, dates, fragments of dreams, and entire sentences struck through with such force that the paper had torn. Once measured and deliberate, his handwriting had tilted sharply, each line more erratic than the last.

Alice turned a page, her fingers pausing near the end. Her face was unreadable in the dim, amber light of the desk lamp. She lingered there, scanning a line, then spoke softly without lifting her eyes. "You're not dreaming about pub conversations anymore."

"Noticing's not enough," Mick muttered, half to himself. "You can spot the fire from a mile off. Doesn't mean you stop it."

Mick paused. He rubbed at his face and let out a slow breath. Though the room was warm, the radiator ticking faintly, he couldn't shake the cold that had worked its way inside him. The words sitting heavy between them. "Last night..." he started, then stopped, finding the shape of it. "Last night, I dreamed half the promenade was missing. Half the street was missing. The buildings, the lights, just gone. Like they'd never existed."

She leaned back in her chair, drawing her hand through her hair, the gesture automatic, distracted. "And when you woke up?"

He glanced past her toward the window. Outside, the streetlights flickered, their glow pale, barely reaching the street beyond. "It was still there," he said. "For now."

The silence that followed wasn't empty. It pressed in, thick and waiting. Mick could feel something creeping closer, not yet visible, not yet explainable, but certain, like the shift in air when the tide pulls further out than it should. "You ever lose something you didn't even realise you'd misplaced?" Mick said. His voice came too low. He thought of the last time Harry had called. The apology he'd never given.

Alice turned back to her laptop. The screen lit her face in quick pulses as she scrolled through folders, opening documents and cross-referencing articles with rapid precision. "Let's compare notes," she muttered. "If things are changing, there must be a pattern."

That was always her way, clinical, meticulous, chasing inconsistencies where others saw coincidence. Even years ago, she'd notice the details no one else did: a pub that swapped names overnight, a neighbour gone without farewell, shopfronts that shifted then shifted back. And when things stopped making sense, she hadn't blamed it on memory. She'd written it down.

Something in her posture changed. Her shoulders drew in, her hand hovered over the mouse. She clicked between two files, frowning. "Here's where it gets weird," she said.

Mick leaned forward as she pulled up an article dated three years earlier about a council redevelopment plan that had been shelved. "I interviewed you for this," she said, her voice low, deliberate. "You went on about Blackpool turning into a stag-do theme park."

Mick shook his head. "I never talked to you about that."

She hesitated, scrolled again. Her face shifted, taking on a darker tone, with less confusion and more concern. "Some versions of this file don't mention you at all."

The words landed quietly but stayed there between them. Mick ran a hand through his hair. His pulse thudded steadily. He kept his voice even. "So, I'm next."

Alice didn't answer right away. Her mouth had drawn into a line. She stared at the screen, then closed the file with a finality that was almost audible. "Not if we figure this out first."

But he could already feel the dull pressure at the back of his mind, the quiet, widening space where parts of himself had once been.

Chapter 8

Mick barely slept anymore. What passed for rest was a kind of limbo. His body inert, his mind adrift, submerged in something heavier than thought. The ache in his joints had settled into permanence, a dull pressure that slowed his steps and dulled the edge of each morning. Nights were no longer a passage toward sleep, but a threshold. A place where waking gave way to something weightier, dense with memory and dread. He had stopped trying to convince himself the dreams weren't real. They clung to him too tightly. As tightly as the smell of smoke that seemed to follow him into waking. The dreams were getting harder to sift. Faces blurred and slid apart. Sometimes, one stayed longer than the rest, a boy with hair that curled at the edges, laughing in a way Mick hadn't heard for years. He didn't want to admit how much he needed that laugh to stay.

Tonight's had been the worst yet. He'd stood on the promenade, the salt air sharp and cold. But another smell cut through it, timber and iron scorched to black. The sky above Blackpool pulsed red. North Pier loomed, skeletal in the firelight. It groaned, deep and broken. Wooden ribs split under the weight of flame, and the sea below heaved, not in protest, but as if to claim it. People ran, some shouting, some silent. Figures flickering in and out of the dark like coals spat from a fire. Then the pier gave one last cry and snapped, falling into the water piece by piece. But the dream didn't end there. He turned from the wreckage, past the shuttered amusements and broken signage, and saw it: another fire. Inland. Still distant. Still worse.

He woke choking on smoke that wasn't there. The air in the flat was thick, unmoving. The sheets clung to his body, sweat-soaked, breathless. He pushed them back and reached for the notebook, his fingers trembling.

Dream: North Pier collapse. Fire. Screams. Second fire, unknown location. Three days.

He stared at the line until the words blurred, then rose, dressed, and stepped out into the cold.

Alice met him outside the Chronicle, takeaway coffee in one hand, the other buried in her coat pocket. Her face was drawn, the skin beneath her eyes grey with fatigue. She looked him over with cautious irritation.

"All right, Holden," she said. "What is it now?"

He didn't answer. Just handed her the notebook.

She read without a word, her mouth tightening, a flicker of something harder than concern showing through. "North Pier?" she said. "If that thing goes down with people on it…"

"It won't be just the pier," Mick said. "There's something else."

She looked at him, squinting like she was trying to see behind the words. "You want to call the police and tell them your dreams say Blackpool's about to go up in flames?"

"They won't listen."

"No. They won't." She tapped the notebook against her knee. "Then we get proof. Details. You said we've got three days?"

He nodded.

"Then let's not waste them."

They arrived at the pier early, before the maintenance crews had cleared out. The sky was colourless, the air damp. Mick leaned against the rail, watching the tide roll in. The structure stood as it always had, tired and sagging slightly, yet intact. Still, the sound lingered in his mind. The groan. The crack. The end of something.

Alice stood beside him, hands deep in her pockets. "In the dream, where does it give?"

He pointed to the far end. "Middle section. Underneath."

"Rot?"

He shook his head. "Didn't feel like rot."

She didn't push. Just nodded and turned back toward town.

The Chronicle's archive stank of glue and paper long past its prime. Alice moved quickly, leafing through clippings with the economy of someone trained to spot what didn't belong. Mick watched her, hands buried in his coat. She paused, pulled a yellowed clipping free.

"Here," she said. "January 1983. Partial collapse at North Pier. Cause unknown."

He read it. Same section. Same vague conclusions. One line caught his breath:

Some witnesses described the sound before the collapse as 'almost alive.'

He exhaled. "That's what I heard. Before it gave."

She looked at him a long time, then slid the clipping into her pocket.

"Then we go back tonight."

They returned after dark. The town had gone still, save for laughter drifting from a doorway and the occasional gull circling bins. The pier stood quiet. Mick placed his hand on the railing. The chill of it sank into his skin. The dream waited just beneath the surface.

Alice raised a recorder. "Let's see if anything's still moving down there."

They stood in silence. The neon behind them flickered, spilling pale colour over the wet boards. A sound came, low and deep, somewhere beneath them, not wind, not tide, but something slower. Like a breath held too long. The hairs on Mick's arms rose.

Alice's hand trembled slightly. "Did you hear that?"

Mick didn't speak. Couldn't. Something was beneath them. And they had three days to find out what it was.

Chapter 9

The cold had settled deep in Mick's bones, but he barely noticed. He sat hunched on North Pier, hands stuffed into his coat pockets, his breath curling in the damp air. The sea stretched before him, flat and endless, swallowing the last of the afternoon light. Below, the tide rolled in beneath the iron supports, constant as breath.

He knew what was coming. Three days. That was all. Before the whole thing went under. He tried to picture the wood snapping, metal twisting, and voices rising in panic before being swallowed by the water. It wouldn't stop with the pier. The town would shift. Whether it believed in premonitions or not.

His fingers twitched inside his coat. He should be doing something. Saying something. But who would listen?

"Penny for your thoughts?"

The voice came from his left, calm, almost casual. His stomach clenched as he turned. The man was already seated beside him. The same one from The Seagull's Rest. The one who had been watching. The one who had vanished before Mick could get a proper look. Now, here he was.

As Mick stood, the world around him shifted, not violently, not loudly.

Across the road, the lamplight flickered and then bent, a crookedness like a broken neck. A shopfront across the promenade blinked between two signs: Blackpool Gifts, Beacon Books, Blackpool Gifts again.

No one around him seemed to notice. Not the couple laughing too loudly at the tram stop. Not the boy kicking at puddles. Mick rubbed at his eyes, but the glitch held for one long, stubborn heartbeat before settling. And he knew then: the cracks weren't just underfoot anymore. They were in the air, the light, the bones of the town itself. He took a breath, held it, and then stared at the man.

Up close, he looked wrong in quiet, subtle ways. His coat, dark and long, hung strangely on his frame, like it had belonged to someone else. His face was pale, drained of colour. The kind of face you'd forget by the time you passed it again. Nothing stood out except the eyes, deep, unreadable, still. Eyes that seemed to have forgotten what they'd seen.

Mick's mouth was dry. "Who the hell are you?"

The man didn't answer. He slid something across the damp bench. A matchbook, worn soft at the edges, the ink on the front faded almost to nothing. Mick hesitated before picking it up. The paper felt fragile. He turned it over. A message. *Find me before it starts again.* Written in his own handwriting. His breath snagged as the matchbook creased in his fist. He looked up. The man was already on his feet, walking away.

Mick shot up. "Oi! Wait…" But the man didn't turn. His steps didn't falter. He moved with an unnatural ease, like time had no grip on him. Mick lunged around the bench, pushed past a small group of tourists. But when he looked ahead, the pier was empty. No alleys. No doors. Just the wide expanse of wet planks, the grey sea beyond.

The man had vanished. Mick turned slowly, scanning the pier, waiting for movement. Nothing. Just the wind rattling the railings and the tide murmuring below. He looked back at the matchbook. His hands were shaking now.

Find me before it starts again.

The ink had smudged. It looked rushed. Familiar. Like it had come from a hand that remembered. The paper was damp. The writing undeniably his. He closed his hand around it and let out a slow, unsteady breath. He had seen strange things before. But this, this was something else. This was impossible.

Chapter 10

Mick sat across from Alice in the dim back corner of The Seagull's Rest. The matchbook lay between them, small and unassuming. The words scrawled on the back stared up at him, waiting. *Find me before it starts again.* He thought about the matchbook, about the moments repeating exactly, about the missing street signs, the wrong headlines.

None of it had the messy, frantic feel of disaster. It felt like editing. A cold hand going back over the day, smoothing the wrinkles flat. Alice tapped a finger against the table, her gaze fixed on it, unmoving.

"So either someone's taking the piss, or you're telling me you wrote this note… before you wrote it."

Mick ran a thumb over the rough cardboard. It felt old. Worn. Familiar.

"I didn't write it," he said finally. "But that's my handwriting."

Alice nodded slowly. "Which means…"

"I'm not just watching this happen." His voice was quieter now. "I'm part of it."

A silence settled. Not hostile, not even shocked. Just heavy, like dust after movement.

Mick had known, somewhere beneath thought, that it would come to this. The dreams, the vanishing faces, the moments replayed exactly as he'd seen them. None of it random. None of it passive.

Alice sat back, chewing her lip. "What if…" She leaned in. "What if you're the reason the changes happen? What if, every time you interfere, it just gets worse?"

Mick's fingers curled around the matchbook. "And what happens if I do nothing?" He nodded toward the open notebook beside him, pages filled with frantic lines. "The pier collapse, the fire, it still happens. This isn't about stopping change. It's about making sure it changes the right way."

Alice exhaled sharply. "And what's the 'right way', Mick? Who decides that?"

Mick didn't answer. He was already pushing back his chair, the matchbook clenched in his hand. Maybe this was what he'd always been good at. Forgetting the things that mattered most. It didn't matter whether it was a son, a promise, or a town. Some things just slid away, easier than they should.

Alice sighed, grabbing her coat. "Oh, of course. And where exactly are we off to now?"

Mick glanced at her. "To change something."

The tram station was nearly empty. A brittle wind swept down the platform, carrying the scent of salt and damp concrete. Mick shoved his hands deeper into his pockets, eyes scanning the space.

He had been here before. Three nights ago. In a dream.

A man in a dark coat was supposed to step onto the platform. He would fumble for his phone. He would drop something, his wallet, maybe his keys, and bend to pick it up. And because of that, he wouldn't see the tram.

The brakes would fail. The tram would hit him at full speed. He would die.

And somehow, that moment, unnoticed by everyone else, would set everything in motion.

Mick swallowed hard. His breath caught behind the noise in his chest. A gust of wind rolled through, pushing at his coat. The air thickened around him as if something waited.

Then, just as the moment arrived, Mick stepped into the man's path.

"Hey, mate…" He grabbed the man's arm.

The man, startled, blinking. "What…?"

And then, the tram screeched past. Not inches from his face. Not in a near-miss. Just… normally. The brakes worked. The tram slowed. The doors opened. People stepped out.

Mick let out a breath. His hands trembled. That wasn't how it was supposed to go. Maybe nothing was supposed to go the way it had. Perhaps that was the point: doing something anyway. Refusing to be the next empty name.

The man frowned, glancing from Mick to the tram. "You alright, mate?"

Mick nodded, stepping back. "Yeah. I just… thought you were someone else."

The man shrugged, stepped onto the tram. The doors slid shut. The moment passed.

Mick turned away. His breath came uneven. He had done it. He had changed something.

But was it enough? What else had just shifted?

Chapter 11

Mick stood at the edge of the pier, the sea thrashing below him, black water frothing against the rusted supports. The wind had picked up, sharp and insistent, pushing at his coat. Above, thick clouds pressed down, the sky so low it felt like the whole world was closing in.

In his pocket, the matchbook felt heavier than it should. He ran his thumb over the edge, tracing the embossed lettering. The words still burned in his mind: *Find me before it starts again.* Mick's stomach turned, a slow, creeping nausea rising as the words settled in. His fingers tightened around the matchbook, the ridges pressing into his skin. A cold sweat prickled at the back of his neck, and his breath hitched, shallow and uneven. It felt like something unseen had just stepped closer.

A sick feeling gnawed at his gut. The first time he had interfered, he'd felt that jolt. The world shifting beneath his feet. And yet, it had worked. The pub hadn't burned. He had changed something. But the weight in his chest told him that wasn't the end of it. It wasn't over.

Back at The Seagull's Rest, he nursed a pint at his usual table, the notebook open in front of him, its pages scrawled with half-remembered fragments of his dreams. Across the room, Alice leaned against the bar, flipping through a newspaper, stealing glances at him between sips of her drink.

"This is mad," she muttered, snapping the paper shut. "You actually think you can change things?"

Mick tapped the page where he had written the date of the pub fire. "I already have. The fire was supposed to happen. It didn't. That means I can do it again."

Alice let out a slow breath, debating whether to humour him or walk away entirely. "Alright. Say you're right. Say reality really is shifting. What's next?"

Mick stared at the latest entry in his notebook. The dream had been vague, fragmented, a man on a bicycle, a tram's headlights cutting through the mist, a dog barking somewhere in the distance, a street sign missing. No fire. No disaster. But what if the small things were just the beginning?

He stood abruptly. "Come on."

Alice frowned. "Where?"

"To test it."

The promenade was near empty, the neon signs of shuttered arcades flickering weakly in the wind. From one of the closed stalls, a faint, distorted arcade tune played on an old loop, its notes fading in and out of coherence. The Big One loomed in the distance, its steel frame barely visible through the mist rolling in off the sea. The air carried salt and something acrid, a thin chemical taint that clung to the damp night.

They stopped at a street corner. Mick checked his watch: 8:17 PM. His dream had been precise. A man on a bicycle would cross the tram tracks. In the dream, the tram had stopped just in time. The man had narrowly avoided an accident. But what if it happened differently?

Alice folded her arms. "Mick, this is ridiculous."

And then, just like in the dream, the cyclist appeared. Dark jacket, hood up, pedalling steadily toward the tracks. Mick's pulse quickened. He took a step forward. The tram's bell rang. The cyclist didn't slow down.

He hesitated for a fraction of a second, his muscles tensing, his mind screaming to move. Then, before he could think better of it, he lunged into the road. His body moved before his mind could catch up, arms outstretched. His hands met cold metal, gripping the handlebars. The cyclist swerved sharply, nearly toppling over.

"Oi! What the hell…?"

The tram screeched to a halt. But something was wrong. Mick's stomach lurched. The tram wasn't where it was supposed to be. In his dream, it had been further back. The cyclist should have had just enough time. Instead, the tram had stopped too soon. And the street sign, the one missing in his dream, stood perfectly intact.

He blinked, his breath catching. Rubbed his eyes. Trying to make sense of what he saw. But the sign was there, solid, undeniable. The creeping wrongness settled in his gut.

Alice grabbed his arm. "Mick."

His breath caught. The dog. The dog had barked in his dream. But now, there was no dog at all. A pressure built behind his eyes, deep and nauseating. The dream wasn't just changing. It was wrong. Like something trying too hard to fix itself and failing.

He let go of the cyclist's bike. "Sorry, mate," he muttered, stepping back onto the pavement.

The cyclist cursed under his breath and rode off, shaking his head in disgust.

Alice watched him go, her jaw clenched. "You saw that, right? That wasn't just…"

"I saw it." Mick rubbed his forehead. The ache was deep, clawing at his skull. "I think… I think it's trying to fix itself."

Alice narrowed her eyes. "It?"

Mick gestured vaguely around them. "Reality. Whatever this is. I pulled something loose. Now it's trying to snap back, but it's tangled."

Alice exhaled sharply. "Jesus."

Mick flipped open his notebook. The dream had changed. He had written about the missing street sign, but it wasn't missing anymore. Which meant something else had changed instead. The pressure in his head sharpened. He somehow knew, with a gut-level certainty, that he had set something else in motion. And whatever it was, it wasn't good.

Back at the pub, he sat silently, staring at the matchbook the stranger had given him. Alice watched him from across the table.

"What now?"

Mick didn't answer because he knew. Because the next dream was already forming at the edges of his mind, creeping in with a sense of urgency that hadn't been there before. Something was coming. And this time, it wasn't a pub fire or a tram stopping too soon. It was bigger. Darker.

His fingers tightened around the matchbook. He hesitated, his breath shallow, his pulse drumming in his neck. What if it had changed again? What if it was waiting to show him something new? Slowly, deliberately, he braced himself and flipped it open.

Inside the cover was something he hadn't noticed before: a second message, faint, as if it had been rubbed away but not completely erased. He held it closer to the dim pub light, his pulse hammering. The words appeared, scrawled in hurried, shaky writing.

You shouldn't have changed it.

A breath caught in his throat. He looked up at Alice. He had made a mistake. And now, something else was happening.

Chapter 12

The matchbook felt heavier than it should. Mick turned it over in his palm, rubbing his thumb along the ridges like a man trying to erase the words etched inside by touch alone.

Find me before it starts again.

And now, beneath that, barely visible in the flickering, battered glow of The Seagull's Rest's ceiling light, a new message, one that hadn't been there earlier.

You shouldn't have changed it.

It wasn't a warning. It was a reprimand. Like a teacher's hand slamming down on a test paper, correcting a wrong answer. The system didn't just erase mistakes. It punished anyone who tried to rewrite them. His pulse jolted. The dull ache that had begun at the tram stop now pressed behind his eyes, a storm not yet broken.

Across the table, Alice tapped her fingers against her pint glass, her gaze sharp beneath the pub's tired light. "You look like you've seen a ghost."

He looked up, mouth dry. "Might've done."

She leaned forward slightly, exhaled. "Alright, Holden. Spill."

He placed the matchbook carefully between them, a lit fuse. Alice leaned in, brow furrowing, reading the words once. Then again. Her mouth flattened. "Shit."

"Yeah," he murmured, rubbing his temple with a thumb gone clammy. "Something's changed. Not just the tram."

Her expression sharpened. "What else?"

He hesitated, thumb flipping through the pages of his notebook, each line familiar but off, his own handwriting twisted in small ways he couldn't explain. "The street sign was back. The tram stopped too soon. And the dog…"

He trailed off.

Alice's brow arched. "What dog?"

He swallowed. He could hear it again, sharp, frantic barking, the scuffle of claws on pavement. Could picture the wiry-haired thing snapping at something invisible, all sinew and nerves. Except it hadn't happened. There had been no dog.

She snapped her fingers in front of him. "Oi. Stay with me."

He closed the notebook with a quiet thud. "Whatever I changed… it didn't stay small."

Alice exhaled through her nose, shaking her head. "Jesus. It's like watching a Jenga tower fall in slow motion."

Mick gave a dry, humourless snort. His hands were damp against the grain of the table. Alice stared at the matchbook again, her fingertip trailing along the edge. "Find me before it starts again." The words sat between them like a dropped weapon.

He leaned forward, voice low. "The stranger. He's the only one who seems to understand any of this."

She followed his glance toward the bar, where Sheila stacked glasses in slow, mechanical motions.

"She knew something, too," Mick muttered. "That night, she served him. Tense. Like she recognised him."

Alice took a long sip from her pint and set it down too firmly. "We need to find him."

"Yeah." The weight of it settled inside him like damp sand. "Before I disappear too."

Alice tilted her head. "You think you're next?"

He didn't answer. Just looked down at the notebook again, where whole lines had begun to fade, the ink losing its shape as if even the page was trying to forget him.

"I don't think," he said. "I know."

They stepped out into the night just after midnight. The sea wind had grown meaner, slicing through the gaps in Mick's jacket, chafing the skin of his neck like a reprimand. The promenade shimmered under a wet sheen, the neon lights from the arcades dragging long reflections across the pavement. Blackpool, after hours, always felt a little more like itself, its painted smiles worn down, its heartbeat sluggish but steady. There was a smell in the air beyond salt and chip fat, something faintly metallic, as though the town was rusting from within.

Alice walked beside him, coat pulled tight, face drawn against the wind. "Where the hell do we even start?" she muttered, not really expecting an answer.

"If he's been around before," Mick said, jaw tight as he scanned the street, "someone's seen him. They'd have to."

They tried the late-night takeaway near the pier, the all-hours off-license where the lights constantly flickered, the taxi rank near the station with drivers half-asleep behind their windscreens. But no one recognised the description. Not the coat. Not the face. Not the stillness. With each blank response, a weight settled deeper in Mick's chest. Frustration built behind his ribs, heavy and slow.

It was only when they passed a row of shuttered amusements, their signs swinging like loose teeth in the wind, that something stopped them. A voice. Calm, disembodied, drifting out from the mouth of a narrow alley. "You're looking in the wrong places."

Mick's steps faltered. Alice's fingers closed around his arm, reflexive. They turned toward the alley, its walls slick with damp, lit only by the streetlamp blinking weakly, not yet dead. Half-shrouded in the gloom, a figure stood against the bricks, arms loose at his sides, the familiar coat hung just as before, unsettling in its precision.

It was him.

The stranger didn't move. Didn't blink. Just watched them with the still patience of someone who had all the time in the world. Alice tensed beside him. Mick could feel her breath shift, a change just beneath her voice when she spoke.

"Who are you?"

The man tilted his head slowly as if examining a detail. "I could ask you the same."

"You know damn well who I am," Mick said, the words scraping out dry.

A faint smile played at the edge of the man's mouth, nothing warm, just the hint of familiarity, of amusement dulled by something heavier. "Do I?"

Mick stepped forward and held out the matchbook. "You left this. 'Find me before it starts again.'"

The stranger's eyes flicked to it but didn't linger. And then, for just a second, something shifted behind them, recognition, perhaps, or regret.

Alice's voice cut the stillness. "What starts again?"

The man finally moved, a subtle shift as he eased away from the wall. "Everything."

It echoed, sharp, undeniable. "That's not an answer," she said, but there was something in her tone, wariness creeping in, doubt folding under the edges of defiance. The man glanced at her, then back to Mick, as if assessing who would last longer. "You're the first one to notice this far in," he said. "That's… interesting."

"What does that mean?" Mick asked, though he was already sure he didn't want the answer.

"You changed something, didn't you?"

"I…" Mick started, but the words caught. His breath felt shallow, like it had to squeeze between the bones in his chest.

The stranger stepped closer, his shoes soundless against the damp pavement. "That was a mistake."

Alice shifted, planting herself slightly in front of Mick without seeming to mean it. "Why?"

"Because now it's not just watching," the man said. His voice wasn't loud, but the words hit with weight, too measured to be theatrical.

The silence stretched. Mick felt it crawling up his spine.

It?

Alice asked what Mick couldn't. "What's watching?"

There was no reply. Instead, the stranger reached into his coat and drew out a small, folded slip of paper. He held it out without ceremony, as though handing over change at a till.

Mick hesitated, then took it. The paper was old, worn soft along the folds. He opened it carefully, fingers stiff.

A grainy photo. His face stared back at him, flat and blurred like it had been printed through fog. Above it, a headline: BLACKPOOL MAN VANISHES UNDER MYSTERIOUS CIRCUMSTANCES. The date below was two days from now.

The night tilted. The air thickened around them. Alice let out a breath that caught halfway. "Mick…"

He looked up. But the alley was empty. The stranger had gone. No footsteps. No retreating silhouette. Just damp brick and the flickering lamp stuttering its way toward darkness. Mick stood there, the paper loose in his hand. He didn't speak. He didn't have to. This wasn't a warning. It was a countdown. And it had already begun.

Chapter 13

The newspaper sat between them on the sticky pub table, its edges curled beneath the weight of Mick's pint glass. The ink looked too fresh. The date at the top ticked forward like a silent bomb. Two days.

Alice hadn't said much since the alleyway. She sat with her arms folded, her fingers hooked around her opposite elbows, staring at the article, willing it to make sense. Her face was tight, unreadable, trying to make sense of the impossible. Mick rubbed at his temple, exhaling slowly. His thoughts were thick with too many pints, too little sleep, and the weight of something pressing behind his eyes. He wasn't just witnessing the shifts anymore. He was causing them. Or maybe... maybe he always had been.

The pub felt wrong around him. Not in the usual way, the usual worn carpets and broken fruit machine noise. It was wrong underneath. Even the air had thinned, stripped of the usual weight of smoke and beer. The dartboard was missing, just a blank square of wall where it had hung for twenty years. The fruit machine had shifted, now facing into the corner like it was ashamed. Even the bar itself seemed longer, stretching unnaturally toward the door. He glanced at Alice, but she was focused on the newspaper, frowning. No one else stirred. No one else saw it. The world wasn't slipping anymore. It was folding.

Alice spoke at last, voice low. "So."

He grunted.

"You were right."

He didn't feel like celebrating.

She tapped the newspaper with one finger. "If this is real, if it's really a report from the future, then maybe we can stop it."

Mick let out a dry chuckle. "That's what I thought about the tram."

Alice's eyes darkened. "Yeah. And that didn't go as planned."

The pub carried on around them, chairs scraping, the low tide of voices ebbing and rising, unaware of the reckoning laid out between pint glasses and folded paper. This wasn't new. He could feel it, deep in the thrum of the walls, the tilt of the street outside. This had happened before. And every time, the world sealed over the cracks a little faster, a little cleaner like a scab pulled too early from a wound. Mick still felt it: the way reality had pushed back. The shift hadn't unfolded like a river changing course. It had jolted. Fractured. Forced. And he knew what happens when you push too hard.

Alice reached for his notebook, flipping through pages already soft with wear. "Alright. Let's break this down."

He raised an eyebrow. "What, like a proper journalist?"

She shot him a look. "Don't." Then, sharper, "We've got two days to figure this out. Unless you want to find out what happens when this headline turns true."

He held up a hand. "Fine. Go on."

She skimmed the pages, flipping back and forth. "You're not just seeing shifts. You're affected by them. Anchored to them, maybe?"

"I don't know," Mick muttered.

She ran a finger along the matchbook beside his glass. "The stranger said you changed something."

"The tram."

"No," she said. "Before that. Maybe even before Gary."

He opened his mouth to argue, then stopped. Something stirred at the edge of memory. The quiz show. The first time he'd known something was wrong.

"What if I changed something," he murmured, mostly to himself, "before I even knew I was doing it?"

Alice's eyes snapped to him. Mick swallowed.

His mind wandered past Gary's disappearance, past the tram, past the dreams that now felt more like premonitions than fragments. Had there been something else? A choice? A nudge? The moment the first thread was pulled? Alice waited. Mick closed his eyes. The headache behind them deepened.

And then, something: a face. Not the stranger. Someone else. Someone he couldn't quite remember. His breath caught.

Alice leaned in. "Mick?"

He opened his eyes. "I think I…"

The lights flickered. The pub dipped, just slightly. The buzz of conversation stumbled and returned. Mick's stomach turned cold.

Alice stiffened. "Did you…"

Mick rose sharply. Something had shifted. It was subtle, imperceptible to anyone else, but he felt it. The seconds were out of order. He looked down. The newspaper was gone.

Alice's fingers twitched. "Mick…"

He scanned the room. The dartboard, the fruit machine, the man behind the bar. All in place. But something had been removed. The article. The headline. Vanished. And in its place, only that tension, that press of something leaning in from the edge.

Then, a voice behind him. Deep. Steady. Inevitable. "You're out of time."

He turned. The stranger stood in the doorway, watching, waiting. This was it. The Choice.

Mick drew a breath. It settled in his chest with the weight of finality. He knew what was coming. Alice did, too. Her hands had curled into fists, jaw clenched. "No," she said. "Not like this."

He gave a tired smile. "No one gets a choice in how it ends, Whittaker."

"The hell they don't."

He faced the stranger, his voice steadier than he expected, resigned, almost amused. "You here to explain, or just watch?"

The stranger tilted his head. "Does it matter?"

Mick snorted. "Not really."

Alice's hands hit the table. "Enough riddles. Tell us how to fix this."

The stranger sighed, slow, almost bored, like a man halfway through a script he'd repeated too many times. "You're not the first to think you could leave footprints in the sand, so you already know the answer."

And Mick did. Courage didn't come easy. Not to men like him, worn thin by bad habits and worse years. But maybe it wasn't courage he needed. Maybe it was just the stubborn will not to give the bloody town the satisfaction of forgetting him quietly. Alice's breath caught. She looked at him, eyes sharp and full of something urgent. "Don't."

He exhaled, eyes still fixed on the stranger. "If I change it one last time, I can stop it."

"You don't know that," she said, her voice softer now but no less fierce.

"I do." He wasn't sure how he knew, but it sat there inside him, immovable.

The stranger said nothing, only watched. Mick turned back to Alice. "If I don't do this, more people disappear. More things go wrong."

There was something raw in her expression now. Anger, defiance, maybe fear. "You don't know what's on the other side of this."

"Maybe that's the point."

She didn't move. Didn't blink. He reached for the matchbook. His fingers brushed it, familiar, final. "Find me before it starts again."

Then he looked at the stranger. "What happens if I do this?"

"You won't be here to know."

He nodded. Not to him. To himself. And he made his choice.

Chapter 14

The world around Mick shuddered, quiet, deep, as if everything beneath the skin of the town had clenched at once. The pub walls, the street outside, even the air itself seemed to tighten, as if the town had drawn a breath and refused to let it go.

Alice felt it, too. She stood rigid, jaw locked, breath sharp and fast. "Mick, don't do this."

He exhaled, slow and deliberate. "Alice, I already have." And as the words left his mouth, he knew. No undoing it now. The shift had begun.

Alice's face twisted, something raw flickering across her expression, anger, disbelief, the stubborn refusal to accept what was happening. She stepped forward, hand half-raised, as if she could still stop him, still pull him back from whatever lay beyond this moment.

"Mick," she tried again, voice cracking, "there has to be another way."

"There isn't." His voice was steady now, maybe for the first time since this whole thing started.

Alice shook her head violently. "No. You don't just... vanish. You don't let this thing take you."

"I'm not letting it take me." He managed a tired smile, weary but sure. "I'm choosing first."

Her breath caught, shallow and unsteady. She wasn't ready. She wasn't accepting this. Not yet. The stranger stood in the shadows, watching without a word. He had always been watching. Mick turned to him. "What happens to her?"

The stranger blinked once, the faintest tilt of his head. "That's up to her."

Alice let out a short, bitter laugh. "Fantastic. That's really helpful."

Mick ignored the cold crawling up his spine. The moment was closing in. The streetlights outside flickered. The walls of The Seagull's Rest felt thinner, as if sound and air might start bleeding through them any second. The world itself was waiting.

He turned back to Alice and held out the matchbook. "Hold onto this."

She stared at it, unmoving. "What the hell am I supposed to do with a matchbook, Mick?"

"Remember."

Her jaw clenched. "No one's going to remember you," she whispered. "Not even me, right? That's what happens?"

He didn't answer. He didn't need to. They both knew.

Alice inhaled sharply, her fingers curling around the matchbook, knuckles white.

He gave her one last look. Not regret, not fear, just quiet acceptance. For a second, just a second, he hesitated. He thought of Harry, not as a man grown, but as a boy clutching a paper trophy, waiting for a father who never came through the door. He thought of Alice, stubborn and sharp-eyed, still standing when the world tried to smooth her down like a crease in a cheap suit. And he thought of himself, the man he might have been, if he hadn't let the weight of forgetting drag him under first. The world wouldn't remember any of it. Wouldn't recognise him. But it didn't have to.

Finally, he turned to the stranger. And he made his move. The moment Mick stepped forward, the world snapped. For a heartbeat, everything held its breath. The faint tang of salt air, the low thud of a dart against wood, all the things that made The Seagull's Rest real, trembled in place. And then they were gone, folded into a silence too smooth to ever have allowed him.

The walls of the pub blurred, the ceiling twisted, and the lights above flickered out one by one. Alice lunged toward him, but it was too late.

Mick didn't fall. Didn't fade. He just... wasn't there anymore. The space where he had stood sealed itself, silent and absolute.

The air stilled. The stranger was gone. And then, everything settled. The lights stopped flickering. The pub solidified. The world clicked back into place. As if nothing had ever happened. Alice stood motionless, pulse hammering, the matchbook still clenched in her hand.

The bar carried on as if nothing had changed. People drinking, talking, laughing. Sheila wiped down the counter, humming under her breath. A fruit machine blinked lazily in the corner. Normal. Ordinary. But the air smelled too clean, too bare. As if the memory of smoke and beer had been scrubbed away along with him. Because for them, nothing had changed.

Alice turned to where Mick had been standing just seconds ago. There was nothing. No chair pulled out, no glass left behind, no trace that he had ever been there.

"Sheila?" Her voice felt too loud, too uncertain.

Sheila glanced up. "You alright, love? You look like you've seen a ghost."

Alice's stomach twisted.

"Mick," she said, voice hoarse. "Mick Holden. He was just here."

Sheila frowned, setting down the glass she'd been wiping. "Who?"

"Mick. Middle-aged, always sits over there, drinks bitter, complains about quiz shows."

Sheila shook her head, genuinely baffled. "Sorry, love. No idea who you're on about."

It hit then. Not suddenly, but with the weight of something that had always been true. The weight of what Mick had done. He wasn't missing. He wasn't dead. He was gone. Erased.

Reality had reset around her. And no one else knew. Her gaze dropped to the matchbook in her fist, her only proof that he had ever existed. She turned it over, fingers trembling. Inside, the writing had already begun to fade.

Find me before it starts again.

Alice swallowed hard. The hollowness inside her settled deeper. Softly, so softly she barely heard it, she whispered, "…Mick?"

There was no answer. She closed her eyes. And everything moved on without him.

Chapter 15

There was not even silence. No hush of breath. No throb of blood. Just absence. Vast, indifferent. Not blackness, not even darkness. Something deeper than either. A space before colour, before sound. It had no weight, no edges. And yet, he remained. Some echo of thought, drifting without form, untethered from time or flesh or anything that could still be called a man.

He couldn't say how long he'd been there. Time had no meaning in that place, no forward, no backward, no measure to cling to. He tried to move, but there was nothing to move. Tried to speak, but the idea of speech had long since become alien. All that lingered was the faint shape of a man who had once been Mick Holden. The name came slow, rising as if dragged from somewhere colder than memory. Was it his? It felt distant, worn-in but not his own. Still, he reached for it. Mick Holden. A man from Blackpool. A man who drank too much. Who remembered how the streets sounded in winter and how the water smelled when it rolled in mean off the Irish Sea. Who'd sat at the end of a bar long enough to become part of the furniture, nodded at by people who no longer recalled his name.

He reached for something else. Alice, maybe. Her steadiness. Her refusal to look away. The way she'd held the matchbook like it meant something. And the pub: the stink of stale beer, the glow of low lights, the gentle clink of glass, that flickering television that never quite found its signal. Those things had weight. They had meaning. They were the last things he had. The last proof he'd ever been real.

Then something changed. Not a sound, not a shift in light. Just a presence. A pressure that circled around him, subtle and deliberate, as if the space itself had suddenly noticed he was still there. It pressed against what was left of him, heavy and patient. Not cruel. Not kind. Just necessary. There was no malice in it. No reason left at all. Whatever had started this process, whatever rules had been set down, they had outlived their makers. Now, it ran on instinct, a machine forgetting its own purpose, smoothing reality because it no longer knew how to stop.

And then a voice, though not a voice as the world understood it, spoke. It didn't arrive on air, didn't vibrate. It settled. Pressed gently against the inside of his thoughts.

You should not be here.

The words were not words, not really. But he understood them. A question rose in him, not formed by tongue or teeth but instinct.

Who are you?

You always ask that.

Had he asked before? The thought came loose, flickered, and vanished. Another instinct rising without shape…

Where am I?

The voice again, the pressure behind it undeniable.

The space between.

Between what?

There was a pause, long enough to feel final.

Before. And after.

He drifted. Not through space, which did not exist here, but through something less precise. Memory, perhaps. Or the scaffolding of memory, the bits left behind after forgetting had done its work.

Somewhere, maybe, there had been architects. Hands that built the rules, eyes that watched the first cracks form. But that was a long time ago. Whoever had started the erasures had long since slipped into the forgetting themselves, ground down by the same slow machinery they set in motion. Now, there were no watchers left. Only the process. Blind. Relentless. Polishing the world smooth because that was all it remembered how to do.

He tried to summon feeling. The cracked vinyl of a bar stool. The heat of a pint glass in a cold hand. The faint, stubborn smell of old beer and salt still clung somewhere, threadbare but real. The matchbook's cardboard, ridged and familiar in his coat pocket. They were still there, just softened, blurred like a dream remembered one morning too late. They were slipping.

The pressure grew. Not angry. Not gentle. Simply inevitable. Ahead of him, just out of reach, was something like a doorway. Not visible. Not open or shut. But pulsing with purpose. Behind him, the world, what remained of it, was closing. Sealing over the tear. Unmaking the space he'd carved by noticing too much.

The voice came again, dull now, like hearing from behind glass.

You won't be the last.

And then another voice. Perhaps the same. Deeper. Slower. More final.

You're not the first.

That was when he understood. The shift hadn't started with him. And it wouldn't end here. But he had stepped forward all the same. Not to be remembered. Not to save anything. Not even to stop it. Just because someone had to. Because something inside him still moved, even now, when everything else had stopped. Somewhere deep, before the crack closed for good, Harry surfaced. The boy he'd failed. The man he'd missed. Mick reached for that memory the way a drowning man might reach for the surface. But it was already sliding, slow and inevitable, into the dark.

The world would seal over him, smooth and final. And no one would notice. But maybe, far above that, some small ripple would remain. Alice might feel it. Someone might. Not his name, perhaps, but the shape he'd left behind. And in that brief, quiet truth, there was something like peace.

Chapter 16

Alice woke to the sound of gulls. Their cries came sharp through the window, scraping across the grey hush of early morning. She lay still beneath the weight of the duvet for a moment, staring up at the ceiling. There was a silence inside her she didn't recognise. Not just the hush of early morning, but something else, the absence of a voice she couldn't quite name, the steady, stubborn presence that should have been there and wasn't. Pale light pressed against the curtains, and from somewhere distant came the churn of the sea, low and irregular, barely audible under the hush. The smell of salt still clung faintly to the air, but thinner now, as if the sea itself had pulled back without her noticing. Not just sleep or loneliness, something shaped like absence. A space someone had left behind.

Her coffee, yesterday's, or maybe the day before's, sat untouched on the bedside table, the top of it filmed over. She blinked slowly. Another morning. Another day in Blackpool. Nothing new. And yet, as she rubbed her face with the heel of her hand, a pressure throbbed faintly behind her eyes, not quite pain, but close enough. It felt like a dream she hadn't fully shaken. There was something off-kilter, a slippage she couldn't name. She sat up, her feet meeting the cold wood floor. Her head ached, not the tight, sharp kind that came from drinking, but a dull internal drag like something had been pulled loose in the night and hadn't found its way back.

She moved through her flat automatically, boiled the kettle, splashed water on her face, opened her phone. No messages. No calls. No notifications of any kind. She stared at the screen longer than necessary, noticing her own reflection faintly in the black glass. She looked tired. Not just tired, out of focus. Like a photo taken at the wrong shutter speed, not quite fixed in the present. She scrolled through her recent calls. Nothing unusual, and yet, something was missing. A name she hadn't called, but should have.

Mick.

Her thumb paused over the empty log. The name should've meant nothing, but it meant everything. It arrived without context, without image, but fully formed. Not just a name. A presence. A voice she hadn't heard recently but should have. A habit no longer there. Her stomach tightened, an involuntary response. She couldn't remember the last time they'd spoken, couldn't even remember the last time she'd tried. Had she? The space where he belonged was too clean, as if something had swept through and taken all the edges with it.

By the time she arrived at the Chronicle, the unease had settled in her chest like something half-dissolved. The office was its usual shape: the low buzz of lights, clicking keyboards, the sour undertone of instant coffee and deadline sweat. She sat down, booted her terminal, and opened the archives before she had time to second-guess why. Her fingers hovered. Then typed: Mick Holden. She hit return.

The screen loaded slowly. When it stopped, there was nothing. No obituaries. No pub quiz reports. No crime notes, council minutes, or one-line quotes from when he'd been drunk and angry about bin collection. Not even a mention. She blinked. Then tried again: North Pier. Pub fire. Disappearances in Blackpool. Still nothing. It was like he had never been part of the town, never sat in those pub corners, never muttered trivia to the telly, never stood beside her, soaked through, laughing at the absurdity of it all.

Outside the office window, the seafront blurred into a soft grey smear. For a second, the clock above the reception desk ticked too loud, then too soft, as if the building couldn't quite decide how time was meant to sound.

She closed her eyes. For a second, she could still hear him, see the way his mouth pulled to one side when he said something sarcastic and low. But even that memory was thinning. Her grip on it slipped the more she tried to hold it. She leaned back in her chair, pressing fingers into her temples. This wasn't just someone drifting from memory. This was someone being removed.

Her coat hung on the back of the chair. She reached into the pocket and felt paper, rough-edged, warm from the lining. A matchbook. She didn't recognise it. The logo was smudged beyond recognition, the corners dog-eared. She turned it over. Opened it. Inside, someone had written: *Find me before it starts again.* She stared at the words. The ink was faded, scrawled in the kind of hand people use when they're in a hurry and scared. And then, even as she watched, the letters began to vanish, faintly at first, then faster. Each stroke of the pen unravelling as if reality itself had changed its mind.

Her chest seized. She grabbed a pen and rewrote the words before the last line faded. *Find me before it starts again.* The ink smudged slightly under her hand. She sat there for a long time, staring at what she'd just rewritten, pulse high in her throat. Something unlocked. Not gradually. Instantly.

She remembered. Mick Holden. The pub. The man in the coat. The smell of smoke, the feeling of being watched, the certainty that the town was slipping under the weight of something it couldn't see. And she knew, without question, without drama, without need for confirmation, that she was not supposed to remember. And now, something, somewhere, knew that she did.

She tucked the matchbook back into her coat pocket. Her voice came quiet, barely more than breath. "I've got you, Mick," she said, voice barely more than breath. The words tasted uncertain in her mouth, but she repeated them, quieter. "I've got you." And she wasn't sure who she was saying it to: him, or herself.

Chapter 17

The first shift was slight. Alice walked the promenade with her coat drawn close. The wind off the Irish Sea cut through the seams of her coat: cold and precise. The sea, slate-grey and twitching, slapped against the stones below. She stopped at the usual corner to light a cigarette, and that's when she noticed it: Hargreaves Off-License was gone. Not closed. Gone.

Where the narrow shopfront had always stood, there was now a smooth, clean, even, indifferent expanse of blank wall. No dusty display, no sun-faded posters offering cheap gin, no crack in the door glass that used to catch her sleeve. She stared, still holding the cigarette, the flame of the lighter forgotten in the wind. Just yesterday, she'd bought a pack of cigarettes here. She'd asked after the old woman behind the till, Marion, or maybe Maureen, and they'd shared some idle remark about gulls tearing open bin bags.

Now, there was no door. No shop. Just wall. She turned, scanning the street. A couple passed her, talking quietly. A bus churned past. In the upper deck, someone was reading the paper. No one noticed the absence. No one hesitated. Only her.

The cigarette fell from her hand, unlit. She didn't bother retrieving it. One gloved hand slid into her coat pocket. The matchbook was still there, edges worn from being turned in her fingers over and over again. The weight of it hadn't changed. And that was the problem. It had begun again. She walked on.

Later that day, in a café near the Chronicle office, she sat at a corner table with a coffee she hadn't touched and the distant static of someone's radio whispering news headlines she couldn't hear. She opened her phone and scrolled through her contacts. Her thumb hovered over a name: Danny Rogers. They'd worked together for years, back when she still thought digging into council reports could make a difference. They'd had a drink last week; Thursday, wasn't it? In the back of The Prince Albert. He'd told her he was thinking of leaving. She remembered the light above their table flickering. She remembered his laugh.

She tapped the number. One ring. Then a flat, clipped message: "The number you have dialled has not been recognised." She checked her text threads automatically. Nothing. No messages. No calls. No history at all. As if he had never been there to reach. She should have been shocked. Should have felt the ground tilt under her feet. But losing Danny felt too familiar. Like the ache Mick had left behind was stretching, growing, swallowing other names, too.

Her chest tightened. She opened her text threads, scrolling quickly, then more slowly, then again. Nothing. No messages. No missed calls. No history at all. As if she'd never contacted him. As if he'd never existed. She set the phone down, pulled out the staff directory on her laptop. Danny wasn't listed. Not under reporters, not under freelancers. Not anywhere.

She scrolled through the staff directory again, slower, as if a name might reappear if she only looked harder. Maybe it was a server glitch. Maybe Danny was sick or on leave. Maybe this was just stress playing tricks on her. She didn't believe it. Not really. But she needed to believe it, even for a minute longer.

She sat there, the coffee cooling beside her, feeling the shape of the absence left behind. Not just the missing number or the blank space in the directory. The joke he never finished telling. The warmth of someone she had known without needing to think about it. If they could erase Danny, what did that make her memories worth? If she forgot him too, would he still be real? Or would he collapse into the gaps with the rest of them?

The matchbook was still in her pocket. Her fingers found it easily, their shape moulded to it now. She didn't take it out. Opening her gallery, she scrolled to the photo from the pub. She was there, mid-laugh, pint in hand. The seat beside her was empty. The table, the window behind her, the other chairs, all there. But Danny, who had been leaning in to make a joke, was gone.

She closed her eyes, then opened them again. Nothing changed. The photo wasn't damaged. It was perfect. Just wrong.

She noticed the third shift at the office. It was subtle, a pause. Paul, her editor, called her over to the meeting room. "Alice?" he said, then hesitated. Barely a second. A flicker of something in his eyes, like a man trying to place someone at a wedding he was not sure he knew. Then he waved her in, back to normal.

She'd seen that pause before. The girl at the café had done it when she handed over the coffee. The man at the off-license. Sheila, too, briefly, behind the bar at The Seagull's Rest. Their eyes would settle on her, just slightly too long. A breath of uncertainty. They didn't know what was slipping. But she did. It wasn't just people being erased. For a second, she forgot the name of the street she'd grown up on. It came back, barely. But the taste of that loss stayed, thick and metallic on her tongue.

It wasn't just streets and names and photos going blank. It was her. The world was starting to forget she belonged to it.

That night, she sat in the half-light of her living room, surrounded by cuttings, photos, and notebooks. Outside, the street was quiet, the usual Blackpool wind rattling half-heartedly against the windows. She flipped through her notes, pausing as something caught her eye. The handwriting was hers, the same pressure and slant, but she hadn't written these words. Scattered between her observations were phrases she couldn't remember recording: *I've done this before. They don't let us remember. Watch the gaps.* And one she did recognise: *Find me before it starts again.*

She turned to a clean page and wrote: *Who else has been here?*

The question sat there, stark, and ordinary. She stared at it. Waited. Nothing.

She sighed, rubbed her eyes, sat back. Then, without warning, the ink began to move. The words she'd written shifted, blurred, the letters folding in on themselves. The sentence faded one letter at a time before reassembling into something new.

You're not the first.

She stared at it. The words didn't move again. Her fingers found the matchbook. It was warm now, impossibly so, as though it had been resting near a fire.

She stood, suddenly needing to move, to do anything, because whatever this was, it had seen her. And if she stayed still much longer, she knew, without drama, without clarity, she'd be next.

Chapter 18

Alice thought about sleeping. Thought about waking to find even more of the world sanded down, maybe even herself. She stayed awake instead, one eye on the clock, daring it to slip. She couldn't go to sleep. Not after the words in her notebook had changed in front of her. Not after the lines she hadn't written appeared in her own handwriting. She'd watched Mick vanish, then heard his voice again in a place he should no longer exist. That kind of thing reorders your sense of what's possible. She needed answers, not just about him. If Mick had left something behind, maybe he wasn't the first. Maybe others had too. Maybe someone had tried before.

The archive room at the Blackpool Chronicle wasn't meant to hold secrets, but it smelled like it did: old paper, dust, damp rising from the floorboards. The bulb above the desk threw out a sickly yellow light, enough to see the shelves nearest the desk and little more. Everything beyond remained in shadow. She hadn't been given the key, not officially, but she'd kept one. Nobody asked. She didn't offer.

She stood in silence before the rows of bound newspapers, waiting for her eyes to adjust. These papers were meant to hold memory, to record the town's petty scandals and minor triumphs. They were proof of lives, even the dull ones. Mick's name should've been among them. She'd checked twice already. It wasn't there.

Her fingers traced the bindings without reading. She wasn't sure what she was expecting, some article she'd missed? No. She'd been looking for Mick. But if they'd erased him cleanly, there wouldn't be anything left.

What if she'd been searching from the wrong angle? What if it wasn't about finding what was there, but noticing what was missing?

She pulled down a volume at random, five years back, and started flipping pages quickly, not reading, just scanning. She wasn't looking for stories. She was looking for holes. Places where stories ended too soon, or didn't begin at all. Paragraphs that stopped mid-thought. Headlines that promised more than they gave. A name mentioned once, never again. An obituary with no photograph and no surviving family. Not blank spaces, but seams, smoothed over by quiet, practised hands. You had to know what to look for to realise anything was wrong. The deeper she went, the more she saw it. Not evidence of deletion, but of repair.

She caught herself turning to ask Mick a question, half out of habit, half out of need. She stopped, hand half-raised, the empty space beside her pressing closer, heavier, as if even her shadow had abandoned her.

They weren't just erasing people. They were stitching over the absences, patching the shape of the world where it had torn. Nothing dramatic. Just tidied away. A crime report without a suspect. A street name changed in one issue, changed back in the next. A council meeting where one councillor's name never appeared in the record. Water had filled the space. The ripple vanished. The surface stilled. But she knew where the stone had fallen.

At the desk, she opened her notebook. She had written in it before, and then the words had shifted. *You're not the first.* She ran her fingertip over the ink. It looked like hers. Felt like hers. But it wasn't. Someone else had written it. Someone who shouldn't have been able to.

Her pulse ticked against her throat. If Mick was gone, gone in a way no one else seemed to notice, then he shouldn't have been able to leave the matchbook. But he had. She flipped through the notebook's pages. The paper felt strange, expectant. As if it knew she was about to ask again. She uncapped her pen and wrote slowly: Who else has been here?

For a second, without thinking, she almost scrawled another name. Mick. The pen hovered. But somehow she knew that even if she wrote it, the ink would thin, and the paper would forget. She set the pen down with a hand that trembled more than she wanted to admit. She waited. Nothing. Of course, nothing. She let the pen fall and leaned back in the chair, her breath easing out. Maybe she'd imagined it. Maybe her nerves had finally twisted themselves into delusion. Then, the words on the page moved. She sat up straight, heart pounding, as the ink blurred, twisted, then rearranged itself: deliberate, steady. The sentence she'd written disappeared. A new one took its place.

Find Harper Ross.

She stared at it, unblinking. The name meant nothing, but her chest tightened anyway, as if some part of her recognised the pattern. She'd never heard it before, had no image to go with it, no place to begin. But it was there. Clear. Precise. Not a warning this time, a direction. A trail. Harper Ross. If the cycle was still happening, if someone else had left a mark like Mick, then maybe they weren't gone. Not entirely. Maybe someone else had made it further. And if they had, perhaps she could too.

She slid the notebook and matchbook into her coat pocket, turned off the lamp, and stepped back into the quiet. The archive room faded into shadow, the scent of forgotten paper still hanging in the air. The name Harper Ross echoed inside her. She didn't wait. She didn't go home. She needed to find them before this trail, too, dissolved into silence. She pulled her coat tighter, but the cold inside her didn't lift. It had worked its way deeper, under skin and bone, the kind of chill that came from too many hours spent awake when the body had already given up on sleep. Her hands shook faintly as she locked the door behind her. When she crossed the empty newsroom, her reflection glanced back from the dark windows, thinner somehow, and half a beat slower to follow.

Chapter 19

In the Chronicle's empty archive room, she started with the digital records. The pale light of the laptop screen painted Alice's face in blue-grey hues, the shadows beneath her eyes darkening with the strain of too many sleepless nights. Her eyes burned from lack of sleep, dry and scratchy, but blinking only made it worse. Somewhere at the back of her mind, a headache built steadily, a slow pressure that blurred the edges of the room. She pressed the heel of her hand against her brow as if she could physically push the ache back where it belonged.

Her fingers hovered over the keyboard, motionless. The room was still. No sound but the low whirr of the fan and the occasional creak from the radiator. The scent of stale coffee lingered, mingling with something older, worn fabric, old paper, the particular dampness that clung to rooms lived in too long and slept in too little.

She typed: Harper Ross. The keys clacked softly. Enter.

The browser stuttered, then filled with a scattershot parade of names, none of them right. She leaned in, scanning faster, the rhythm of it burning into her fingers. Too many Harpers, too many Rosses. None of them hers. She leaned in, elbows pressed to the desk, eyes scanning the screen with that tight, forensic rhythm that never really left her. Something about the name pulled at her: not recognition, exactly, but a sense of proximity. As if the words had passed too close once, brushing her skin in the dark. She couldn't place it. A name from a case? A byline? A scribble in the corner of a page? She scrolled faster, hunting.

There were no social media hits. No trace in public records. A few scattered mentions, a Harper Ross quoted in a local council complaint from Norwich, another mentioned in an obituary in Glasgow. All wrong. Just fragments. Shadows. Then came the silence. Not the absence of data but the kind of stillness you notice in a house that should be full. Like a house that had been quietly cleared out. Alice rubbed her palm slowly along her thigh, not to soothe but to confirm she was still here, still solid. Still real. She typed her own name. The letters wavered, shapes she recognised but didn't trust. For a breathless moment, she didn't know if she was spelling it right, or if she ever had.

Alice searched again for Harper Ross. She narrowed the filters. Blackpool. One result. A digitised newspaper clipping. Old. Crooked. She clicked.

A Vanished Story. The archive listed it under Local Interest – 1997. The scan loaded with a delay, as if resisting. The image tilted in the frame, its edges browned with age. There was a photo, grainy, black, and white. Not a face. Just Blackpool's promenade, taken at a slant. Empty benches. Overcast sky. Early morning or late evening, it was hard to tell. The headline read:

Missing: Harper Ross, Last Seen Near North Pier.

Her breath caught. She read the short article aloud.

"Harper Ross, 27, was last seen leaving a local pub on the evening of October 14, 1997. Witnesses report seeing her walking alone toward North Pier just after midnight. She has not been seen since. Police investigations have yielded no significant leads."

Harper Ross had vanished the same way Mick had. Slipped between cracks the town didn't even bother filling. She wondered if Harper had felt it too, that loneliness so sharp it hollowed you out, left you echoing with names no one else could remember.

That was all. No follow-up. No photo of the missing person. No mention of family, workplace, friends, none of the scaffolding that usually surrounds these things. It felt clinical. Not just absent of details, but scrubbed of them. As if someone had passed a cloth over the history and left only this faint residue.

She scrolled further, watching as the last few lines of the article dissolved into blur. Not digital noise, not compression, something else. The words had been removed. Not hidden. Removed.

Nearly thirty years ago. And now the name, Harper Ross, was appearing in her notebook, as though from behind something she'd only just noticed. She leaned back in her chair, slow, steady. Reached for her phone. 2:47 a.m. She should sleep. Let it sit. Come back to it with a clear head.

But she wouldn't. She knew that already.

The Chronicle kept physical records, boxes of old print files and clippings no one had touched in years. The paper trail might still hold the truth even if the digital archive had been altered. Or the part of the physical archive that hadn't been erased yet.

No more waiting. She wasn't chasing ghosts anymore. She was following a trail left by someone who might have already stood where she stood now. She was going to meet Harper Ross, wherever she was.

Chapter 20

The Chronicle's archive room had a stillness that wasn't peaceful. It was the kind that clung to the skin. Outside, streetlamps hissed against the damp windows, casting fractured yellow lines across the cabinets. Alice stood in the doorway, bathed in the cold glow of her phone screen, breath shallow, heart working too hard for the quiet around her. She wasn't meant to be here. Officially, the archives closed at six. Unofficially, the spare key had never been asked for, and she had never volunteered it. She had moved through the darkened newsroom like a trespasser. Desks turned to shadows, monitors black, the after-hours quiet, not restful, but empty in the wrong way. She let the door shut behind her and waited for the soft click of the latch, then stood still for a moment, letting her eyes adjust.

The air carried the dry, metallic tang of dust and brittle paper, with something beneath it, residual heat from long-dead electronics, the ghost of cigarettes smoked decades ago, and the faint, sour trace of damp. She moved down the line of cabinets, fingers brushing cold steel, her eyes scanning the curled tape labels. When she reached the drawer marked 1997, her stomach tightened. She opened it, slow and careful, the runners shrieking faintly in protest, and the smell of old ink and decaying paper rose to meet her. The motion left her dizzy. She steadied herself against the metal cabinet for a moment, willing her vision to stay sharp. Her limbs felt heavier than they should, each movement dragging against an invisible weight. The floor underfoot seemed to tilt, just slightly, as though the room itself was unsure of its shape.

Inside: neatly folded clippings, yellowed at the edges, with newsprint that had survived longer than most of the stories it recorded. She thumbed through headlines. Crime reports. Petty council squabbles. A heatwave in August. Carnival photos. Then she saw it. The name. HARPER ROSS – STILL MISSING AFTER ONE MONTH. Her breath hitched. She slid it free and stepped back, letting the drawer rest open, the cold metal brushing her hip. This version was longer than the one online. Older, less edited, more human. The photo was grainy. The face blurred by time.

"Harper Ross, 27, was last seen near North Pier on the night of October 14, 1997. Witnesses reported seeing them acting strangely in the days leading up to their disappearance, mentioning forgotten conversations, misplaced objects, and an increasing fear that something was 'watching' them."

Alice felt a tightening low in her abdomen. A quiet, bodily recognition, not fear, exactly, but the confirmation of something she hadn't wanted to believe. She kept reading. "Friends described Ross as a private but meticulous individual, known for keeping detailed notebooks. One acquaintance, who declined to be named, said Ross had been 'writing things down so they wouldn't be erased.' Others dismissed the behaviour as stress or paranoia." That line stopped her. The words felt too familiar. Notebooks. A compulsion to record. She glanced at the article again, then turned it over.

The final paragraph had been torn away. Not folded, not worn, or faded, ripped. A jagged edge where the paper had once continued, the last few sentences surgically removed. Alice stared. Her first thought wasn't panic. It was curiosity. A sharper, deeper question: who had done that, and what had they needed to remove? It wasn't just carelessness. Someone had taken the end of this article with intent. She tucked the clipping into her coat, folded once, not creased, and reached to slide the drawer closed, then paused.

The rest of the 1997 clippings were gone.

Every other file. The dividers were still in place, the labels untouched, but the space behind them gaped hollow. The realisation didn't land all at once, it seeped in, slow and inevitable.

She hadn't noticed before. Had assumed the drawer was full. It wasn't just that the files were gone. It was that something had remembered they needed to disappear. Harper's article had been missed or left behind.

Something shifted. The silence inside the room changed. It wasn't a noise. Not quite. But the quality of the air altered, too still, too expectant. The smell of old paper sharpened. Alice rubbed her arms, trying to shake the sensation, but the feeling dug deeper. She turned slowly. The room looked the same. The door remained shut. No movement. No sound. But her instincts pulled tight, like a story resisting the telling. She needed to leave. Her legs resisted at first, the heaviness pulling at each step. Walking became conscious, mechanical, like trying to move underwater.

She crossed to the door quickly, not rushing, not running. She wouldn't give whatever-this-was the satisfaction. She put her hand on the handle, turned it. As the door opened, something brushed the edge of perception, not a voice, not a whisper, but a pressure against her chest, low and intimate. A phrase, not spoken but understood. Not heard but left behind like dust in her lungs.

You're getting too close.

She didn't look back. Didn't stop. She stepped into the newsroom. Behind her, the archive door clicked shut. But the pressure didn't lift. It followed, weightless but certain, like breath waiting just behind her shoulders.

Chapter 21

Alice hadn't slept. Not after the whisper in the archive, not after the torn edge of the newspaper where the final paragraph should have been. She sat at the kitchen table long after the streetlights had clicked off and the cold light of dawn had begun to seep between the buildings. A fresh notebook lay open in front of her, her pen idly turning in her fingers. Outside, the road was slick with last night's rain, bins already rattling as a refuse lorry groaned its way down the street. She felt suspended, as if time had stopped ticking forward and now hovered uncertainly around her. The newspaper fragment rested under her coffee mug, the words barely legible in the greying light.

Harper Ross. A name, a vanished person, an itch she couldn't leave alone. What was left of them could be carried in a jacket pocket. A name wasn't a life, but it was a place to start.

Alice began the way any rational person would, with the records. At the central library, she fed coins into the old microfiche reader and rolled through dim rolls of type. The noise it made, like a tired machine straining to remember, filled the reading room with a steady hum. She checked the electoral roll, the town archives, old registries written in fading municipal ink. She found nothing. No address. No listed job. No family connections. The kind of absence that suggested more than simple oversight. Harper Ross had lived here. That much she knew. She had vanished in 1997, last seen walking toward the North Pier, carrying a notebook and muttering to themselves.

But the town had swallowed them clean. She rubbed her temples and stared at the blank space where their name should have appeared in the registry. This wasn't someone who had slipped between the cracks. This was someone who had been scraped out entirely.

In the late morning, with her head buzzing from library air and too much vending machine coffee, she walked to the King's Arms. It was one of the oldest pubs in Blackpool, the kind that smelled of soaked timber and unwashed carpets. The same three pensioners sat in the back corner under a wall-mounted TV tuned to the racing channel. The room was thick with silence, broken only by the hum of an old fruit machine and the clink of pint glasses being emptied slowly and with purpose.

She ordered a drink she wouldn't finish, bitter, the sort of thing that lingered in the mouth, and approached them with the casual politeness of a stranger hoping to pass unnoticed. They glanced up, curious, perhaps wary. She smiled lightly and asked whether they'd been drinking here long, which was like asking if they'd been breathing long. One of them snorted, told her he'd been coming since before decimalisation.

That was good, she said, because she was researching something for the Chronicle, something old. A name. Harper Ross.

It was subtle. The way the air shifted, just slightly, as though the room had inhaled and forgot how to exhale. One man blinked slowly. The oldest rubbed at the side of his nose. Then, confusion. Not the blank kind that came from age, but something else. A deliberate not-knowing. The name had landed and bounced.

Harper who?

She repeated it. Ross. Used to drink in places like this. Always had a notebook. Bit of a loner, maybe a bit off. The second man shook his head slowly. The third muttered that she had the wrong person. She sipped her pint and watched their eyes, saw the flicker, just for a second, of something uncertain. As if they had heard the name before, but the memory of it now curled and slipped from their grasp like smoke. They didn't look evasive. They looked edited.

She tried another angle. What about missing persons? Anyone from that time, back then, who just disappeared? It was the kind of question old men in pubs usually loved. The soft nostalgia of mystery, someone vanishing into the past. But again, there was the pause. A slight creasing of the brow, something tugging at the corners of thought. One of them frowned, but it was brief, too brief, and then his expression cleared, suddenly blank. "Nah. Don't think so."

Alice sat with that for a moment. She left a few coins for the drink and stepped back into the street, which by now had brightened into a weak midday. The light glared off wet pavements, and the gulls screamed above the rooftops as if offended by her presence.

She went to other places. Another pub. A café where older men played dominoes in silence. Another pub, its windows painted shut against the daylight. She asked. She listened. She watched the same pattern repeat, curiosity, hesitation, a flicker of memory struggling to push through, and then nothing. The details weren't just gone. They were being overwritten in real time. And that, more than anything, made her skin crawl. It felt alive. The forgetting. It moved against her thoughts, like a tide slipping backwards. The more she pushed, the more it receded.

By evening, the rain had returned, gentle but steady, pattering against the brim of her hood. She walked along the promenade with her coat pulled tight, unsure of where she was going, only that she wasn't ready to stop. The town was nearly empty. The arcades shuttered, their flashing lights dulled behind glass. The ice cream kiosks were locked and dripping. Gulls huddled under eaves and watched her pass without interest. The wind smelled of salt and metal and something older. She didn't know why she stopped when she did, just a flicker of instinct.

There was a small booth near the entrance to the North Pier, its paint flaking, its fortune-teller sign swinging gently in the wind. The windows were plastered with yellowing scraps of paper, pinned in overlapping layers like a madman's diary.

Most were nonsense. Cryptic phrases. Strings of numbers. Single names with no context. But as she stepped closer, something shifted in her gut. Not fear. Not recognition. A wrongness she could feel before she could see it. A name. Not Harper Ross. Her own. Alice Whittaker. The ink was faded, the paper thin from moisture. She reached out and lifted the note. It weighed nothing, yet her arms dragged as if against water. Beneath her name, three words.

You found me.

That was all. She stared at it, her breath turning shallow. The paper was older than it should have been. Too old. As if it had waited here for years, decades, through salt wind and winter frost, for her to arrive and see it. And now that she had, something in the air had shifted. She turned slowly, scanning the length of the pier, the gulls, the shadows.

There was no one. And yet someone had known she would come. Someone had left this message, not for just anyone, but for her. Harper Ross, perhaps. Or someone further back, older still. She felt a chill settle behind her ribs and realised she hadn't exhaled. She slipped the note into her coat The air around her felt thinner, stretched too tight, as if the town itself had paused to see what she would do next. She walked away from the pier without knowing where she was going next. But she knew this much. She wasn't alone anymore.

Chapter 22

The rain had returned, thin but unrelenting, that fine northern kind that blurred the world without announcing itself. It tapped softly on the warped planks of North Pier, a quiet, needling sound that might once have been comforting but now only deepened the silence. Alice stood motionless in its rhythm, her fingers stiff with cold, the soaked paper trembling slightly in her grip. She had read it three times now, though she didn't need to. You found me. That was all it said. Nothing more. The ink had faded to a dull grey, the edges browned by time, as if the years themselves had scorched them. It felt old in a way that defied time. Not just aged, but expectant. And though it made no sense, none of this made sense, some part of her knew the message had waited for her, and only her.

She turned her head, slowly, instinctively, and found herself staring at another fortune teller's booth a few paces away. The glass window was crowded with scraps of paper, a chaotic collage of messages left behind, some in neat cursive, others a frantic scrawl, many blurred into ink smears by salt air and rain. She stepped closer, boots creaking against the soaked wood, the hem of her coat dragging along rusted bolts and frayed rope. Most of the notes meant nothing. Numbers. Single words. Names half-remembered or never known. She scanned them, not knowing what she was looking for, only certain she'd recognise it when it appeared.

Folded near the fogged corner of the window, barely visible beneath the condensation, a phrase emerged, familiar in a way that unsettled rather than reassured. She slid the glass open and retrieved the note with cautious fingers. The paper tore slightly, disintegrating under her touch.

Find me before it starts again.

The same words Mick had found. The same ones from the matchbook. Her breath caught. The chill of the pier pressed deeper, not from cold, but from recognition. Someone, long before her, had stood in this same place and left behind a breadcrumb, hoping it would be found. She folded the note and slipped it into her pocket, then turned away from the booth, eyes scanning the length of the pier. Wind howled through the rusted iron framework above, whistling through the gaps where banners once hung. The sea below churned dark and restless, its voice low and constant. And somewhere out there, beyond the water and the brittle wood beneath her, Harper Ross had vanished.

She moved slowly, stopping often. She checked beneath benches slick with moss and salt, ran her fingers along the flaking paint of the railings and the splintered beams. A few gulls lingered overhead, hunched and indifferent. Nothing moved. The pier was dead, but not silent. It breathed through rusting joints, sighed with the memory of footsteps long since faded. It felt less like a place and more like a held breath. She found the third note beneath a bench, wedged between two warped boards. The corner of it curled upward as if reaching toward her. She crouched and pulled it free.

Not just us.

The words bled together, blurred by time, but the meaning held. Harper had not been alone. Others had known. Others had tried. And none of them had mattered. Alice stood there for a long time, the note soft in her grip, and folded it before slipping it into her pocket beside the first. A cold certainty settled beneath her ribs.

The rain was heavier now, though still quiet. It soaked through her coat, flattened her hair to her scalp, ran down the back of her neck in slow rivulets.

Twenty minutes passed in a blur, her boots slick with rain, her breath clouding as she walked. She found the next note wedged inside a rusting ticket booth, the paper curled into the metal.

Remember.

Her throat tightened. She was trying. She was remembering things no one else could or would. And the further she moved along the pier, the more it felt like memory was the only thing keeping her tethered to the world.

She didn't stop. Another note emerged behind the frame of a faded sign pointing to amusements long since shut. This one was longer, its edges curled and darkened by time.

The first time, I thought I was losing my mind. The second time, I knew I was. The third time, I understood. It doesn't matter how many times we fight it. We all make the same choice in the end.

She read it once, then again, the words sinking in with a quiet inevitability. The paper felt warm despite the cold. She pocketed it and moved on.

Near the carcass of an arcade machine, the kind that once blinked with coloured lights and warbled out tinny music, she found another, folded tight, jammed between rusted panels and almost invisible to the eye. She pried it out with her nails.

You think you're solving it. You're not. You're just the next one to try.

The rain had seeped into the ink, but the sentence held. Her hand clenched around the paper. There was no grand revelation waiting. No code to crack, no door to unlock. A fog of understanding settled over her, not sharp, not sudden, but dull and absolute. There was no puzzle. No escape. Just repetition. Mick had not been the first. Harper had not been the first. And she, Alice, was not the last.

The end of the pier loomed ahead, where the planks turned darker still with damp, slick with moss, and the sea stretched out in a wide, indifferent sprawl. She walked toward it with deliberate steps, unhurried, unafraid. The metal railings trembled in the wind. She crouched beside the benches, ran her hand along the supports, fingers sliding over bolts slick with rust, scanning the warped platform as though the wood itself might give up its secrets.

No paper. No message. But her fingers caught on something else, something rough, unnatural, resisting the grain. She leaned closer.

Carved into the timber, barely visible beneath the years of salt and weathering, was a sentence etched in uneven strokes.

It will be your turn next.

She drew back, slowly, and without thinking reached for the matchbook. Flipped it open. The words were still there: *Find me before it starts again.*

Softened by rain. Blurred at the corners. But intact. She stared at them, her breath shallow, as if reading them aloud in her mind might draw something closer. There was always something left behind. Not just signs. Not just paper. But shape. Structure. The cycle wasn't theory. It wasn't madness. It was design. Etched into things. Embedded in the physical world in fibres, ink, wood, and habit.

She stood with care, squaring herself against the wind. The air around her seemed thinner now, as if the pier itself had drawn a breath it didn't plan to release. She wouldn't follow the same path. She wouldn't vanish into someone else's footsteps. If she was next in line, she would choose differently. She scanned the shoreline, the crumbling silhouettes of buildings, the blinking lights dulled by the mist, and let the thought settle.

There was one place left to search. She didn't know what she would find. Only that something had been left for her, something Harper had hidden, something Mick had missed. And if it hadn't been scrubbed clean, if the world hadn't quite reached it yet, then it would be waiting. And she would find it. Before it started again. Before it reached her.

Chapter 23

The wind off the sea had turned sharp by the time Alice left the pier, a cold that didn't just bite but burrowed, slipping through the seams of her coat and settling deep into her bones. She didn't notice. Or perhaps she did and simply didn't care. Her steps were fast but not hurried. She wasn't escaping anything; she was moving toward something. The words she had collected, the warnings, the confessions, the fragments of people who had vanished, replayed in her head like a whispered chorus.

Not just us. Remember. You're just the next one to try. It will be your turn next.

Each one chipped away at the fragile surface of her certainty, not because they were cryptic, but because they were true. They hadn't been left as riddles. They were memories, left like bloodstains on the walls for someone who might care to see them.

Harper Ross had been here before her. Not just here in this town or in this pattern, but in this exact state of mind, standing at the edge of understanding, already too far in to get out cleanly. The clues weren't about finding a person. They were about retracing an unravelling.

She went first to the town Registrar's office, knowing what she was looking for before she arrived.

The place was silent in the way only council buildings can be, a silence made of heavy doors, dry air, and a staff that had long since stopped expecting anyone to care about the past.

Alice didn't ask for help. She found the electoral records for 1997 and combed through them with the quiet determination of someone looking for a name she already expected to see. And there it was. Ross, Harper. 16 Kingsley House.

Alice's breath came fast, but not with excitement. This wasn't discovery; it was confirmation. This was where it had ended for Harper. If anything remained, it would be there. Alice didn't pause to consider what she was doing. She didn't check the time. She simply left, leaving the file still open on the counter, walking out into the wet light of Blackpool's afternoon, already halfway to Kingsley House in her mind. Outside, the town moved as it always had, tired, indifferent, eyes turned inward. No one noticed her leaving. No one would notice if she didn't come back.

The building stood just past the decaying conservative club, squat and red-bricked, with damp crawling up its edges and a sense of tired resignation in its architecture. Kingsley House wasn't pretending to be anything it wasn't. Alice stood outside the entrance, facing the intercom with its faded, peeling numbers. She scanned the panel. Flat 15. Flat 17. No Flat 16. Just a blank space between. She pressed the buttons anyway, knowing it was pointless. Nothing answered. She checked the postboxes, each one bearing a name she didn't recognise. No Ross. No trace of a Flat 16.

She stepped back, staring up at the building, counting the windows. There was a gap. A section of wall where a window should have been. Where one had to be, but there was nothing. A solid patch of brick where, structurally, a window needed to exist. Alice's hand went instinctively to her pocket, fingers wrapping around the matchbook like it might anchor her to something solid. She stood a moment longer, then turned and moved down the side of the building into the narrow alley behind it.

The alley was thick with the sour smell of rotting rubbish and old rainwater. Bins overflowed beside rusted drainpipes, and puddles reflected a fractured, discoloured sky. Alice walked slowly, her eyes scanning the back wall of the building, searching for something that didn't fit.

And there it was. A door. Half-hidden in shadow, old and rusted, with no number, no handle plate, nothing to suggest it was in use.

She stepped closer. Something had been scratched into its surface, almost invisible beneath layers of peeling paint. *Find me.* The words made her breath catch. She reached for the handle and turned it.

Locked. Of course.

She stepped back, exhaled through her nose. And then she saw it, a single brick missing from the wall beside the door. Just a gap. She crouched and reached in, her hand brushing something cold and metallic. A key. She didn't hesitate. She slid the key into the lock. Turned it. The door opened with a sound like something exhaling after a long time buried.

Chapter 24

She hadn't meant to stay. But once the door closed behind her, she knew there was more here than just dust and forgetting. The dust in Harper Ross's flat hadn't just settled. It gathered. In the corners, along the seams of the warped floorboards, it thickened in the absence of breath, of movement, of life. Alice didn't touch anything as she entered. She had no need to. The air told her all she needed to know: no one had been here in years, perhaps longer. It was the kind of silence that pressed against your chest, made the walls feel too close, as though they were listening.

The room around her felt smaller. The darkness pressed inward; the air grew heavier, thick with the sense of something shifting unseen. She turned sharply, heart hammering, half-expecting someone to be standing behind her. But there was only the warped floor, the cracked walls, the silent bed.

She sat at the desk without a sound. The chair creaked beneath her, not loudly, but enough to draw her back into the moment. She switched on the torch on her phone and placed it gently on the surface, letting the beam fall across the notebook that lay there, untouched, waiting. Her fingers hovered over the first page. The light trembled slightly. She realised her hand was shaking.

The first entries were precise. Controlled. Neat rows of handwriting, each line carefully measured, as though order itself might be enough to stave off whatever had begun.

There was a kind of rhythm to the notes: quick observations, dates, simple sketches in the margins. The marks of someone who had spent their life shaping chaos into story. Harper had been a journalist. Alice could see it in the way she had constructed her evidence, each thought boxed in, held still.

The first line stopped her cold.

First time: a word out of place. Second time: a missing object. Third time: someone who was there... wasn't.

Alice's lips pressed together. That was how it had begun for her, too. A forgotten mug. A conversation that didn't happen. A face in the pub, then not. She turned the page. Faster now. The entries gathered pace with her.

Reality is not stable. But no one else sees it. At first, I thought I was misremembering things. But it's not my memory that's broken. It's the world.

She paused. The light flickered slightly as the phone adjusted to the dimness, its beam sliding across the grain of the wood, catching on the rings left by old cups. The quiet of the room was absolute. Her own breathing, steady now, filled it. She turned the next page more carefully. The handwriting had begun to slip. Where once there were tidy lines, now there were loops written sideways, words squeezed into the corners, fragments crossed out and rephrased with increasing urgency.

When something disappears, it doesn't just vanish. The world corrects around it. The past changes. The gaps are stitched up. But I remember.

Alice's throat tightened. It was like flinching at her own unfinished reflection.

Another line: *If I don't write things down, they slip away.* Then, beneath it, the one that stayed with her even as she read on: *People hesitate when they say my name. I am being erased.*

She turned another page, and this one had been circled so many times the pen had almost torn through. The words were heavier, carved rather than written.

This has happened before. There are others.

And then the next page. A list. A simple list of names. Most of them were crossed out. The pen marks were brutal, decisive, not the kind of strike-through made in error but with finality, like the names themselves had been overwritten. She scanned them slowly, each one unfamiliar, until her eyes stopped. One name, left untouched. Mick Holden.

A prickling sensation ran along the back of her neck. She hadn't met Mick when this had been written. She hadn't even known he existed. And yet here he was, uncrossed, recorded long before they had crossed paths. As if Harper had seen him, somehow, through the fog that was gathering now around Alice's own life. It wasn't just a pattern. It was a cycle. Mick had been caught in it long before Alice understood she was standing on the same ground.

The next pages fell into a kind of frantic delirium. Ink bled across corners, half-started sentences crossed out mid-thought.

They know I see it. It's getting worse. My flat, but the rest was gone, smudged beyond recovery. I tried to warn them. They don't remember the warnings. The world REWRITES THEM.

Alice felt it in her chest then, a dull pressure, not fear exactly, something else. Recognition. A quiet dread that had no sharp edges. She turned another page and found it nearly blacked out. The ink pressed over itself, again and again, layers of panicked correction. But in the bottom right corner, left untouched: *If you're reading this, you already know what happens next.*

She didn't move for a long time. That sentence: she had known it was coming. But seeing it, in Harper's hand, carved out of time and shadow, made her grip the edge of the desk.

Alice knew. Of course she knew. It had already started.

She turned the final page. No ink. Just the grain of the paper cut deep by something sharper than a biro. The words weren't written. They were gouged.

There is a way out.

She ran her finger along the groove, almost expecting it to be warm. It wasn't.

The room closed in around her. The torch caught dust in the air, trembling. She snapped the notebook shut. Harper had known. Not just the danger, not just the erosion, but something more. A direction. A thread through the maze.

Alice stood slowly, slid the notebook under her arm, and reached into her pocket for the matchbook. She opened it and read the words inside again, the ink fading, the edges soft from weeks of being folded and unfolded.

Find me before it starts again.

She wasn't leaving it here. Because Harper Ross hadn't disappeared. She had been waiting. Somewhere past this apartment, past the erasures, past whatever rules governed the crumbling edge of reality, she was still there. Alice had found the place where Harper had last existed. And she wasn't going to stop now.

She turned back toward the door, notebook clutched tight. Harper had left her a map. She just hadn't drawn the road. But Alice would walk it anyway. She didn't know yet where it would lead. Only that it would start with Mick, and maybe, if she was quick enough, if she was right, just maybe, it wouldn't end with her. Not this time.

Chapter 25

Alice's fingers trembled slightly as she tucked Harper Ross's notebook beneath her arm and looked around. Once dense with presence, the flat now felt curiously absent, stripped bare by time, memory, and the kind of vacancy that left a trace. Dust hung thick in the air, blurring the light from the window into dirty streams. What furniture remained looked defeated: a sunken chair, a table with a thin skin of dust, a teacup stained with age, still sitting on the windowsill. The silence was not peaceful. It was watchful. She wasn't done here.

The last page was missing. Not torn in haste, not worn by time. Removed. Neatly, deliberately. A choice, not a mistake. Something had ensured that whatever Harper had written last, the conclusion, the reveal, never made it into the world. But Alice didn't believe in perfect disappearances. Something always lingered. A smear of ink. A curl of tape. A fingerprint on the underside of a drawer. The world could try to cover its tracks, but it never managed to be as neat as it wanted to be.

She stood in the middle of the room, letting her eyes move across the space. The air carried the dull scent of closed places: paper, stale water, the faint mould where the walls met the floor.

The wallpaper lifted in corners, curling like dried leaves. Damp had crept up where the plaster sagged. An unplugged kettle sat on the counter in the kitchenette, its surface dulled by neglect.

Harper had lived here, and perhaps she hadn't left, so much as dissolved. The only thing that felt even remotely used was the desk, and even that looked like it had been abandoned mid-thought.

She opened the drawers: they slid out with a rasp. Empty. She tapped the bottoms gently, listening for hollow spaces. Nothing. Then, crouching low, she reached under, her hand sweeping along the wood until her fingers caught on a strip of something brittle. Tape.

She peeled it away with care. A small piece of paper came loose, curling at the edge as it came free. Two words, hastily scrawled.

Not here.

A warning? A note? Harper hadn't destroyed the missing page. She'd moved it. Somewhere safer. Somewhere, the shift hadn't reached.

Alice rose, knees stiff. The room tilted slightly, the walls stretched too tight, and she reached for the bookshelf to steady herself. The books leaned at odd angles, a mixture of old novels, notebooks, academic texts, some collapsed, others stubbornly upright. She scanned them slowly. Then she saw it. A gap. Rectangular. Clean. A shape where something had once rested, now claimed by dust. A book had been removed. A hiding place. Not recently. Long enough for the air to forget.

She pressed her fingers into the dusty space, holding them in the outline of the missing object. Whoever had taken it they had known exactly what to look for. And yet, if Harper had hidden it there, it meant intention. It meant Harper had left a path.

Her hand dropped away from the shelf. She turned again, slower now, thinking. Not the pier. Too exposed. Not the Chronicle. Too obvious. Harper had hidden things in places people didn't notice, under tables, under floorboards, carved on beams. Places that didn't draw attention. Places always there. Never seen. She closed her eyes. And it came to her. The Seagull's Rest. Mick's spot in the corner. The one people avoided unless no other seat was left.

She didn't remember leaving the flat. Only the rain beneath her boots, the sharp cold tightening her breath, Harper's notebook pressed close to her side. By the time she reached The Seagull's Rest, the damp had crept into her coat, and the edges of her mind felt blurred as if waking from a dream.

Inside, the pub was quieter than usual, shrouded in the hush of low conversation and clinking glass. The television above the bar flickered with a muted football match while the smell of greasy food and stale beer thickened the air, heavy as damp cloth. Behind the bar, Sheila wiped a glass with the rhythm of habit. She looked up, her expression neutral.

"Back again?" she asked, not unkindly. "Didn't think this place had anything left for you."

Alice stepped to the bar slowly. She kept her voice even. "Did Harper Ross drink here?"

There was a pause, not long, but enough. Sheila's hand stilled. Her eyes tightened, not with suspicion, but with the discomfort of something unfamiliar trying to find a place to settle. "No idea who that is," she said, too smoothly.

That was enough. Alice gave a slight nod and turned away, her boots making a soft scrape on the worn floorboards. The pub looked the same, the same tables, the same scattered regulars, the same wear on the rugs, but the air felt thick, the walls stretched too tight. She crossed to the booth in the corner. Mick's booth. Harper's, maybe. It no longer mattered.

She slid into the seat and felt the cushion sag beneath her weight, familiar, yielding. She ran her fingers under the table, found nothing. Pressed into the seams of the cushion, still nothing. Then she glanced up. The beam above was stained dark from years of smoke and time, but etched faintly into the wood, a word had been scratched.

Look.

She stood on the seat, one hand braced against the wall for balance, and reached. Her fingers brushed a thin edge, paper, taped to the top of the beam. She peeled it free with care. The tape cracked softly as it came away. The page, once folded, had grown brittle with time; the ink had turned to a brownish grey. The message, brief, waited in her hands.

There is a way out. But only one of us ever makes it.

She stood there for a moment longer. The note fluttered faintly, but the words pressed into her chest like a hand. No surprise. No confusion. Just confirmation of what she already knew. Around her, the pub carried on in its usual rhythm. Laughter at the bar, someone shifting in a chair, the mechanical blink of the fruit machine cycling through empty patterns. She stepped down, slipped the note into her pocket, and walked out without a word.

The air outside had turned colder. Wind pushed in from the sea, tugging at her coat, flattening her hair against her cheek. Far off, down the dark promenade, a gull cried once, sharp and distant. She didn't look back. There was no need to. The wind pushed against her, steady and insistent, like a hand at her back. The booth, the message, the withheld truth all had settled into something inevitable. She had a decision to make now. And the weight of it was growing by the minute. Whether she followed Harper's trail or broke from it, she wasn't sure yet, only that she was closer. And that the worst part might not be choosing. It might be discovering what had already been chosen for her.

Chapter 26

The promenade was nearly empty. The sky had settled into its usual grey, the kind that made no distinction between morning or evening, and the wind rolled in off the Irish Sea with a damp insistence. Alice walked without direction, hands sunk deep into her coat, the folded note pressing against her hip like a bruise. She hadn't read it again, there was no need, but the words looped, caught somewhere behind her eyes. *There is a way out. But only one of us ever makes it.* She didn't know what disturbed her more: the finality of the statement or the calm certainty in its phrasing. Whoever had written it hadn't been afraid. Or perhaps they had simply accepted that fear didn't change anything.

She stopped near North Pier, drawn not by thought but by the gravity of familiarity. It was where Harper had ended, or begun, or disappeared, depending on who, or what, you believed. The sea below crashed against the rusted supports, not angry, not gentle, just indifferent. The metal railing was cold beneath her hands, damp with sea salt and time. She leaned forward slightly, the wind curling beneath her collar. Something about this place, about the silence between the gusts, suggested that Harper had stood here too. Maybe not on this exact plank, but close enough. Maybe she'd gripped the rail the same way. Maybe she'd felt the same dull certainty gathering behind the ribs, the way fog gathers before the sea vanishes entirely. Alice could feel it now. The knowledge she hadn't wanted. The realisation she'd chased without admitting it to herself. The pattern didn't end. It just chose someone new.

She pulled out the matchbook without thinking, as if her hands needed to move. She flipped it open, already knowing what she would see. *Find me before it starts again.* It no longer felt like a message. More like a reminder. A phrase left behind by someone who had understood the rules a little too late. She stared at it for a moment, then wondered, for the first time, truly, who had written it. Was it Mick? Harper? Someone before both of them, long gone and long forgotten? Someone the world had already scrubbed clean, not just from memory but from reality itself? She thought that was the worst part, not dying, not vanishing, but the idea that it might happen so completely that no one would even notice.

The wind shifted. She could taste the salt now, sharp on her tongue, and she found herself gripping the railing harder. The message from the note returned again. *Only one of us ever makes it.* And she began to wonder, had Mick taken Harper's place? And if so, was she now set to take his? Was that the price of escape? Was she willing to pay it? She didn't know what scared her more, the idea of being replaced or the idea of becoming the thing that replaced someone else. Her stomach turned, hollow and cold. She pressed her hand to her coat pocket, to the notebook. Harper's notebook. Still here. Still solid. Still, proof that someone had existed before her. The pages inside were thick with names and half-memories and the slow, uneven documentation of something that moved faster than understanding. She had come so far looking for a flaw in the pattern, some crack in the wall that might let her slip through without consequence. But now it was clear there was no flaw. There was only the choice: take your turn, or become part of the silence.

She spoke aloud though there was no one to hear her. "What if I don't choose?" Her voice came out quieter than she'd expected. "What happens if I refuse?" The waves offered no answer, just the constant, tired rhythm of something that had always been and always would be. She wasn't expecting a reply. And yet, there it was. Not a sound, exactly. Not a voice. A presence. A pressure. Not in her ears. Not in her mind. Somewhere else. Somewhere between.

You already made your choice.

She turned sharply, instinct taking hold, eyes sweeping the empty pier. But no one stood there. No figure. No movement. Only the groan of steel and wind through the support beams. Yet she wasn't alone. Not truly. Something was watching, not with eyes, not in the usual way. But it was watching just the same. Waiting. For her to do what was already written.

Her breath caught in her throat. She pulled the notebook from her coat with deliberate fingers as if speed might summon something worse. She opened it to the older pages, to the ones marked in Harper's neat, spiralling script. Mick's name appeared again and again. Places. Times. Notes about shifts and disappearances. A map of something larger than either of them, half-sketched and fraying at the edges. She turned the pages slowly. Then she saw it. A single line, almost lost beneath a hurried scrawl.

Did I escape? Or did I just forget?

She stared at it for a long time. The letters blurred and reformed, blurred again. It wasn't a question. It was a sentence already passed. This wasn't a game you won. It was a loop you endured. It was never about breaking the pattern. It was about recognising when it was your turn to vanish. She closed the notebook with care as if it might dissolve in her hands if she wasn't gentle.

She felt the weight of the wind, the cold railing against her back, the matchbook warming again in her pocket. She thought of Mick. Of Harper. Of the names that no longer appeared in any record. The ones that had slipped just far enough into the silence that no one remembered to ask where they'd gone. And then she thought of herself. Alice Whittaker. The last one left. Still here, for now.

She could walk away. Pretend none of it had happened. Let herself slip quietly into the rhythm of the town. She could become a ghost with a name on a mailbox, nodding at people who no longer remembered who she was. Or she could go forward. Not to solve anything. Not to win. But to finish it. Even if it meant being the one who didn't make it.

Her fingers curled around the notebook. The decision had already been made. Maybe not in this moment, but long before. Maybe by someone else. Maybe by her. It didn't matter.

She turned from the sea, the wind at her back, the weight of the matchbook still present in her coat. And stepped into whatever was waiting. Behind her, the air seemed to fold in, closing the space where she had stood.

Chapter 27

Alice had spent days chasing ghosts. Not the kind that drifted through walls or flickered at the edge of vision, but worse, the kind that vanished from memory, from paper, from rooms that used to echo with their names. Mick. Harper. The ones the world seemed determined to forget. She'd followed clues that unravelled themselves, questioned people who remembered too little, and walked streets that shifted beneath her. But something had changed. Something inside her had settled. She was done flinching every time the world bent sideways. Done reacting. That hadn't worked. Now, she would act. Pull at the seams until the fabric gave way. She didn't expect to win. She didn't even expect to understand. She just knew it was time.

She began with Sheila. The Seagull's Rest hadn't changed. Still dim, still quiet, still steeped in the smells of old lager, cracked upholstery, and fried things long since scraped off plates. At this hour, the pub was half-asleep. A few drinkers hunched over their pints, the loyalty of men who no longer drank for company. The radiator behind the bar hissed and clicked, swallowing water. Sheila stood where she always did, wiping down a glass that didn't need wiping, her cardigan sleeves pushed to her elbows, her dyed hair flattened by the damp. Her eyes narrowed as Alice walked in, but not with surprise, only a kind of weariness. "Another late one, then?" she said, not really asking.

Alice didn't answer. She slid onto the stool at the corner, closest to the register. She didn't order, didn't reach for a menu. She leaned in, not loud or dramatic, and said, "I know you remember."

Sheila blinked. "Remember what?" Her voice had the faint edge of caution, a tone she used on customers who came in talking too fast.

Alice held her gaze. "Harper Ross."

There, just the slightest change. Not confusion, not recognition, something in between. A tightening behind the eyes, like a door rattling on its hinges.

Sheila opened her mouth, then closed it again. "I don't know who…"

"Yes," Alice said, calm as a whisper. "You do."

She reached into her coat and pulled out the folded newspaper clipping, the one that wasn't supposed to exist anymore, the one she had rescued from the archive like a corpse that had been buried too shallow. She unfolded it on the bar and slid it forward. The paper was yellowing now, creased where her fingers had pressed into it, but the words remained. Sheila looked down.

She didn't gasp. She didn't cry. She froze, her hand hovering above the glass she'd been wiping. Then, after a long moment, she brought her fingertips to her temple, massaging a spot as if trying to press something loose from inside her skull. Her eyes closed. Her jaw clenched. Alice leaned in, not urgent, not hopeful. Just tired. "Fight it." A beat passed. Then another. The fruit machine clicked softly in the corner, then fell silent as though waiting.

Sheila opened her eyes. She didn't look at Alice. She stared at the clipping, her face blank except for a single tremor in her bottom lip. "Bloody hell," she whispered.

Alice said nothing. She waited. Sheila didn't lift the paper. She just looked at it, silent, searching for something already lost.

"She came in a lot," she said, finally. Her voice was different now, slower, less guarded. "Didn't talk much. Always had a notebook. One of those little ones, elastic round the middle. She'd sit in the back. Same seat every time. Sipped at her drink like she was just trying to make it last." Alice nodded once. "She was scared," Sheila added more quietly.

"Kept saying things weren't right. That people were... going. Not dying. Just gone." She shook her head. "I told her she needed rest. Or help. Or both." She paused again. "She said it started at the theatre."

Alice leaned in slightly. "The Grand?"

Sheila shook her head. "No. The Winter Gardens."

That landed like a weight between them. Alice knew the place. Everyone in Blackpool did. A building that couldn't quite forget what it had once been. It still had the bones of glamour but none of the skin. Ballrooms that smelled of mildew and echo, corridors that bent at the wrong angle, windows that reflected things they shouldn't.

"She say what she found?" Alice asked.

Sheila took a moment. Then: "Only that it didn't want to be seen."

Alice exhaled through her nose. That was enough. Harper had left a trail, and it led there. But she wouldn't follow it unarmed. Not this time.

The Chronicle building was dark when she arrived. Streetlamps lit the bricks a sour yellow. A few office windows still glowed faintly down the block, but hers were dark. She let herself in, not bothering with the lights, just the small desk lamp that left more shadows than it banished. The building smelled of paper and wire and the faint, sweet rot of forgotten lunches in forgotten drawers. She sat, fingers resting on the keyboard. For a moment, the hum of the building seemed to stutter, as if the place itself resisted what she was about to leave behind. Then she typed:

If anyone finds this, my name is Alice Whittaker. I am investigating the disappearances of Mick Holden and Harper Ross. Reality is shifting. The world is erasing people. If I go missing, it wasn't an accident. Start at the Winter Gardens.

She printed three copies. One she taped to the underside of her desk drawer. One, she slipped into the archive room between two files that hadn't been touched in years. And the last, she folded into an envelope, sealed it, and wrote her name in block capitals on the front.

A breadcrumb. A reminder. Something to anchor her if the forgetting reached her too.

The printer groaned as it settled back into silence. Somewhere above, something creaked in the pipes. She put on her coat and stepped back outside. The night was colder now, the streets empty, windows shuttered. The kind of cold that got into your bones. She didn't stop walking.

Chapter 28

The Winter Gardens rose out of the dark like something half-remembered, its facade caught in the tired amber spill of the streetlamps. The ironwork above the doors was ornate once, now rusted and pitted by years of salt air. Its great glass dome sagged under bird droppings and grime, throwing back broken reflections of the empty road. Alice stood at the edge of the pavement, her coat pulled tight, breath curling white into the night. In her pocket, her fingers curled around the matchbook. Small enough to forget, but it anchored her more than she'd admit. Harper Ross had come here. And now, so would she.

She didn't bother with the front entrance. Locked doors were theatrical, meant to suggest importance. Instead, she circled to the side, where the town turned its back on the building, slipping past bins and broken signage to the loading dock with its rusted railing and forgotten crates. Most of the windows here were boarded up, the paint flaking from their sills like old skin. She found the fire escape, narrow and brittle-looking, but still solid underfoot. One hand on the metal, the other gripping her coat, she climbed. No thought, no pause. Just breath, effort, breath. At the top, a pane of glass had been punched out. She swung one leg through, then the other, the crunch of her boots against the flooring loud in the stillness. The moment she landed, she flicked on her torch. Dust curled in the beam like smoke from a cigarette.

The building didn't just feel abandoned. It felt sealed off from time. Untouched, not merely empty. She stood in what had once been a grand Art Deco entrance hall. Faded posters for shows no one remembered peeled from grimy walls. A velvet curtain, stained and sagging, clung to a brass pole. Yellowed ticket booths lined the wall, silent and obsolete. She took one step forward. The click of her boot echoed once, sharply. Then again, softer. And then a third time, too slow, out of rhythm. She stopped. Listened. The phone felt heavier in her hand, its light dulled. She told herself it was nothing, but waited longer than she needed before moving again.

She passed through the foyer, past a bar stripped bare, its shelves empty, its mirrors cracked and dusty. The smell of mildew clung to the walls, layered with something older: old wood, maybe, or the ghosts of cigarettes smoked decades ago. A door to the Pavilion Theatre hung half-closed, as if someone had slipped through without caring to pull it shut. She pushed it open.

The theatre swallowed her. Rows of seats stretched into darkness, dust-blurred and sagging. Overhead, a chandelier, improbably intact, swayed gently, though no breeze moved the air. She swept the torch across the room. Light skittered over faded velvet, caught on the edge of the stage, but revealed nothing. Still, the skin on her arms prickled. The theatre felt expectant. Not just empty, waiting.

She moved down the aisle. The carpet, damp and dead underfoot, muffled her steps. At the edge of the stage, she climbed up slowly, feeling the boards flex under her weight. She turned and looked back toward the seats. For a moment, she saw them filled. Not with people exactly. With presences. The shape of Mick. Of Harper. Of others whose names she had found but never dared speak aloud. Watching. Waiting. She blinked hard. The image clung longer than it should have.

She turned toward the wings. There, slumped behind a fallen curtain, a narrow door stood ajar. She crossed to it, brushing the heavy fabric aside, fingertips grazing the wood. The light from her torch barely caught the frame. Beyond it, only blackness. She stepped through without a sound.

The corridor beyond shouldn't have been there. She knew it instinctively. The proportions were wrong, the ceiling too high, the walls narrowing too quickly. The darkness pressed in, thick and heavy, swallowing the beam of her torch. She turned, expecting to find the doorway she had come through. But there was only blank wall, smooth and featureless. No hinges. No frame. The cold here wasn't the cold of the outside night. It was deeper, older, the kind that seeped up from beneath foundations and forgot to leave.

Still, she walked.

Overhead, a few strip lights still buzzed, uneven, failing. Between them stretched long corridors of shadow. Her steps slowed without meaning to. She kept to the centre, wary of brushing the walls. The torch flickered, then steadied again. The silence was different here. Layered. Listening.

At the far end of the corridor, a figure stood. She stopped. The figure didn't move. It was tall, motionless, little more than an outline against the jittering light. She raised the torch. The beam slipped around the shape as if repelled by it, unable to fix it into view. Her breath quickened. She found her voice, though it came smaller than she intended.

"Harper?"

No answer. The figure shifted, not stepping forward, just a slight rebalancing, as though it had aligned itself more precisely to the dark. She didn't move. The cold had reached her chest now, not chill, but thinning, like the oxygen itself was being peeled away.

The torch flickered once. Then again. And then she heard it. Not from ahead. From beside her. Low, intimate, in the breath just beyond hearing.

"You're too late."

The light died. Something shifted at the edges of her vision, a feeling of being untethered, even before the ground gave way. The floor gave way beneath her. Alice fell, soundless, into the dark.

Chapter 29

For a moment, there was nothing but pressure, the ghost of a fall still pressing against her ribs. Alice opened her eyes to nothing familiar. Concrete stretched beneath her palms, cool and gritty, and the air hung thick with dust and the flat, mechanical tang of oil, or perhaps just the stale breath of a room sealed too long. She stayed still, letting her body catch up, her thoughts falling back into sequence. No pain. No alarms blaring in her mind. Just the quiet, dislocated certainty that she wasn't in the Winter Gardens anymore. She knew it immediately, the way you know when a dream ends even before your eyes have opened.

She sat up slowly. The weight in her skull throbbed with a dull, rhythmic insistence, not pain exactly, but pressure, gathering behind her eyes. The ceiling above flickered under tired industrial bulbs, their yellow light stuttering in jerks. The pitted concrete walls gave nothing away. One door, rusted and sealed from her side, waited ahead. No windows. No vents. No clues.

She rose, moving her hands instinctively to her pockets. Empty. No phone. No notebook. No matchbook. Just the coat on her shoulders and a hollow space inside her where certainty used to live. She pressed her fingertips into her palm until it hurt, the small pain anchoring her. She was still here. Still Alice Whittaker. For now. She didn't hesitate. She moved to the door and pushed.

The hallway beyond stretched long and grey, lit by flickering bulbs that seemed too tired to hold up the darkness.

The hum of electricity was faint, uncertain, as if the building itself doubted its existence. Alice walked slowly, her boots striking a soft echo off the concrete that felt too loud. She turned a corner and stopped.

It wasn't strange. It was worse than strange. It was familiar.

The Blackpool Chronicle office. Or something that looked enough like it to fool someone who wanted to believe. Desks in rows. Chairs tucked neatly under. Filing trays. Keyboards. But no fingerprints. No coffee stains. No clutter. The smell gave it away first, too clean, sterile, a set dressed by someone who had never been inside a real newsroom. She moved forward with deliberate steps. Every desk was the same. Perfect. Dustless. Memory replayed, but without the living details.

Then she saw her desk. The chair was pushed back slightly, as if someone had just stood up. But the desk itself was bare. No half-written stories, no mug ring, no battered pen. No trace of her. She stood there for a moment, waiting without knowing what for. Then something tugged at the corner of her mind. She turned.

Across the room, a figure watched her. A woman stood near the far wall, tall, wrapped in a dark coat too heavy for indoors. Her face caught only the edge of the flickering light, a mouth, a browline, little more. Alice moved forward, her heartbeat thick in her ears. The woman mirrored her exactly, each step measured, silent, deliberate. Alice stopped. So did she. The air between them tightened, strung taut as wire. Alice cleared her throat, her voice dry and cracked. "Harper?"

The woman blinked once, slowly. Then lifted her arm and pointed. Alice followed the gesture. A door had appeared. Plain. Wooden. As though it had always been there, waiting for her to notice. She turned back. The woman was gone. Not vanished in movement, simply no longer there, as if she had never been real.

Alice hesitated for one breath, then stepped to the door and pushed it open. The shift was immediate. Heat rushed at her. Noise crashed over her. She stumbled forward onto sticky, varnished floorboards. The heavy scent of beer, sweat, and stale grease filled her throat. She caught herself against the back of a chair, blinking hard.

The Seagull's Rest.

The dartboard thudded somewhere across the room. Glasses clinked at the bar. A burst of laughter broke from a nearby booth. The world had returned in its full, shabby weight. And yet. She reached into her coat pocket.

The notebook was there. The matchbook too. As if she had never left. As if none of it, the concrete, the empty office, the woman, had ever happened. But she knew better. Her body remembered. The heavy silence. The airless dark. The way time had slipped sideways.

She flipped open the matchbook. The message inside had changed. *Not much time.*

She closed it slowly. Slid it back into her coat. Around her, the pub continued as it always had. The same uneven floor. The cracked mirror behind the bar. The same faces, a little too worn, a little too settled. But something had followed her back. She hadn't returned alone.

Chapter 30

Alice sat at the back of The Seagull's Rest, the matchbook resting lightly between her fingers. The pub's evening rhythm ebbed and muttered around her: the clatter of a pint set down too hard two tables over, the low current of conversation, the smell of stale beer and old grease that lived in the grain of the wood. Above the bar, a football match flickered on a muted television, the picture stuttering faintly, dissolving into the atmosphere. Everything was familiar. But not the kind of familiar that comforted. It felt posed. Touched-up. A world trying too hard to seem real.

She flipped the matchbook open with her thumb.

Not much time.

Three words, faint, but rooted now so deep into the paper it seemed they would never leave. She closed it again slowly, her gaze lifting without moving her head. Sheila stood behind the bar, talking to a man whose face didn't settle in Alice's memory. Near the dartboard, three old men threw in lazy arcs, murmuring among themselves. A couple sat near the window, not speaking. Everything looked normal. But underneath, something strained. As if the walls themselves were holding their breath.

Alice slipped her hand into her coat pocket and drew out the notebook. The pages gave easily under her fingers. She turned to a blank one and wrote her name.

Alice Whittaker.

She stared at it, waiting. As if the letters might shudder, rearrange themselves, betray her.

They didn't. The ink stayed steady. She let out a breath she hadn't known she was holding and turned the page.

The words waiting there were in her handwriting but not her hand, slanted, urgent, pressed too deep into the paper:

It's watching. Don't let it know you see it.

Her stomach tightened. She looked up, slower this time.

The air hadn't shifted. The pub looked the same. Yet something had entered the space, as surely as a storm front slipping in unnoticed. She saw him then, a man in a long coat, sitting alone in the booth near the far wall. Still. Unmoving. His presence was too clean to be casual. Too precise. Watching her.

She reached for her pint glass, sliding her fingers around it as though nothing had changed. Took a careful sip. Her eyes stayed fixed on the television, catching the flicker of light across the bar's mirrored shelves, across Sheila's hair. In the corner of her eye, the man did not blink. He did not drink. His hands rested lightly on the table, unnaturally still. As if he wasn't part of the room but something stitched into it. The longer she ignored him, the heavier his attention pressed against her, a slow, deliberate weight. Not hostile. Not curious. Just present.

Without looking, she opened a new page in the notebook. In her smallest, tightest hand, she wrote:

Who are you?

What do you want?

She waited, the page open beneath her hand. The pub's noise continued, normal on the surface. Someone laughed too loudly behind her, a dart thunked into the board, but the world under it had shifted.

Then her hand moved.

Not involuntarily, she felt her fingers, knew it was her own body, but it was as though the decision had already been made. The pen scratched once against the paper, spelling out a single word.

Run.

She looked up. The booth at the far end was empty.

No man. No coat. No pint. Only the dull red vinyl of the seat, smooth and untouched. Her heart began to beat harder. Not in fear. In certainty. She glanced down again.

Run.

Still there. Not a warning. A command. Whatever had come back with her, whatever had slipped through the fractures of the night, it was already here. And it wanted her to move.

She closed the notebook and slipped it back into her coat with steady fingers. She rose slowly from her seat. The floor under her boots felt solid enough. She didn't look back. She didn't need to.

She stepped toward the door, into the thick cold waiting outside. The streets would be empty. The sky low and damp. And somewhere out there, the thing that had crossed with her would be waiting.

It had given her the first move. And she made it. But not the one it expected. Because if it was waiting for her to run, then running was the last thing she would do. She was going to find it first.

Chapter 31

Alice walked away from The Seagull's Rest without looking back, her footsteps steady against the slick pavement. The air had turned colder, heavy with the salt of the sea and the faint burn of wet concrete. The lights behind her dimmed one by one, swallowed by the fog curling in from the promenade. She knew it was behind her. Not chasing. Not following. Just there, the weight of it pressed between her shoulder blades like an old instinct, a pressure that said something had noticed her and would not let go.

It wasn't in a hurry. It didn't need to be. It was waiting, patient, certain she would falter first.

She didn't.

The matchbook dug into her palm, the cardboard edges anchoring her better than any resolve could. She wouldn't run. Not this time.

She crossed the tramlines, the town around her half-lit and indifferent, its windows smeared with the soft weight of sea mist. Her feet carried her without thought toward North Pier, where the town's heartbeat slowed to a hush. The off-season stillness wrapped itself around the planks and iron railings, a deliberate abandonment. Built for laughter once, now left to rot.

The boards groaned beneath her weight, hollow and reluctant. The wind hunted through her coat, tugging at the seams, fingering its way down the back of her collar. She passed the shuttered amusements, the dark arcade stalls standing silent, and settled onto a bench halfway down the pier. The sea stretched before her, black and wide and unknowable.

She sat without glancing back. No need. She waited, letting the silence stretch thin, letting whatever followed her decide what came next.

Her fingers, stiff with cold, slipped into her coat. She pulled out the notebook, flipping to the last page. Her own handwriting stared back, a single word hastily scrawled.

Run.

She uncapped her pen, moving carefully despite the tremor that edged her hands. Beneath the warning, she wrote, slow and steady:

I'm not running. Show yourself.

She shut the notebook and laid it beside her on the bench. Leaned back. Breathed. The sea hissed beneath the boards, the wind caught in the slats, whispering as if from another room. She counted under her breath. One. Two. Three. A breath sounded behind her. Or the imitation of one. Thin, flat, without warmth.

"You shouldn't have done that."

She turned. It stood a few feet away, still and expressionless. The dark coat hung from its frame, heavy and outdated, the kind worn in photographs yellowed with age. But it was the face that undid her. Mick's. Or close enough to unsettle. The lines of his mouth, the tilt of his jaw, familiar, but blurred at the edges, softened like wax too close to heat. The eyes were worst. Smooth. Blank. As if drawn from memory, not life. Alice stood slowly. Her voice came steadier than she expected.

"You're not him."

The thing tilted its head. Not confusion. Recognition.

"You brought me back," it said. Mick's cadence, but hollow. A mimicry.

She didn't blink. "Who are you?"

The answer came flat, without pause. "You already know."

And she did. The pieces settled around her, not sudden, just inevitable. Harper's warnings. The missing faces. The rhythm of disappearance and replacement.

"You're the gap filler," she said quietly. "The patch. The thing that holds the seams together."

It said nothing, only smiled, faint and deliberate.

"That's why Mick vanished. Why Harper disappeared. You took their place."

The smile widened. And in Mick's eerily familiar voice, it said, "Your turn."

Her body reacted before her mind caught up. The matchbook was already in her hands, her fingers moving fast. She flicked it open. The words inside twisted before her eyes, shifting.

Not much time.

Then:

Burn it.

She struck the match. The flame flared, struggling against the wind. The thing stepped back, not far, but enough. Enough to know she was right. She cupped the flame with both hands and brought it to the matchbook. The fire kissed the paper and raced across it faster than it should have, hungry as petrol.

The thing shuddered. Its expression changed, not anger. Not pain. Something smaller. Older. Fear. It opened its mouth but made no sound.

The air folded around it, and the world lurched, pulling back as if to escape what had been stitched into it. And then it was gone. The coat. The face. The mimicry. Only a curl of smoke and a small heap of ash at her feet.

Alice stood breathing hard. The cold rushed back, clean and honest. The kind of cold that belonged. She crouched. The ashes fell apart under her fingers, weightless. All of it gone, except for one scrap of paper, a sliver barely large enough to carry three words.

Not the last.

She closed her eyes. The matchbook had burned. The thing had vanished. But the cycle hadn't ended. Only paused. Skipped. Waiting.

She stood slowly, letting the wind lift the scrap from her fingers. It tumbled away over the pier's edge, swallowed by the black sea. The night thickened around her, the sea a restless murmur at her back, but the town's lights still stitched a crooked path behind.

Then she turned. Her shoulders stiff, her breath slow. Blackpool loomed ahead, quiet and smeared with mist, its distance wide and indifferent. If this wasn't over, then neither was she.

Chapter 32

Alice stood at the edge of North Pier, the wood slick beneath her boots, the sea a heavy mass of grey beyond the railings. The wind came from all directions, curling into her coat, tugging strands of hair across her face. She let it. Somewhere below, the last ember of burnt paper twisted once before the waves swallowed it.

She had burned the matchbook. Ended something. Not all of it. The memory of the matchbook's last whisper clung to her, coiling tighter the longer she stood still. The silence that followed carried weight. Not relief. Not resolution. Just the echo, faint but persistent: *Not the last.* It rang in her skull like a whisper left behind in an empty room.

She breathed sharply. The air was sharp as vinegar, briny, raw. It clung to the back of her throat. She could leave. The thought hovered, as it always did, simple as stepping through an exit door. Forget Mick. Forget Harper Ross. Forget the glimpses she'd seen of people who shouldn't be there. Bury it. Pretend she hadn't seen the cracks.

But the trouble with pretending was simple. Once you saw them, really saw them, you couldn't go back. The same face twice in a crowd. The clock that reset itself. The stranger who remembered your name before you spoke it.

She clenched her fists inside her pockets, pressing fingertips deep into her palms until she felt the slow, stubborn thud of her pulse. She already knew. She wasn't walking away. Not this time.

The council archives were housed in a low concrete building, few people noticed unless they had to. It crouched at the corner of two roads, heavy, mute, its windows tired with grime. She had passed it a hundred times without thinking. Now it felt inevitable.

She broke in at 3:42 a.m., that hour when the world forgets its own shape. The back door lock had rusted to the point of surrender. A twist with a screwdriver she had grabbed from home, and she was inside.

The air was thick with damp plaster and the sour odour of cleaning chemicals. Fluorescent strips buzzed overhead, half of them blinking, making the shadows jump in tired, uneven patterns. Cabinets lined the room in long rows, grey on grey, their labels dulled by decades of dust.

She moved slowly, fingers brushing along the metal. Births. Deaths. Property. Elections. And there, halfway along the far wall: Missing Persons – Pre-2000.

Her heart knocked once inside her ribs. She opened the drawer. The files were warm, heavy with time, their spines bowed, their paper yellowed and soft. She flipped through: names faded, faces forgotten. A catalogue of erasures no one had cared enough to contest. Then she found it.

Frederick Langley. Missing, 1962.

She pulled the file. The paper inside smelled faintly of mildew. The report was clipped neatly, the language clinical.

Subject reported episodes of déjà vu. Misplaced time. Inconsistencies in memory. Claimed the world was "correcting itself" around him. Final statement before disappearance: "It's my turn."

Her hand froze over the page. The same pattern. Sixty years earlier.

She turned the next page. A photograph, paperclipped at the corner, its edge rusted. A man in his thirties. Coat collar turned up. Expression unreadable under flat, careless light. Him. The man from the pub. From the platform. From the pier. Always on the edge of things. Always almost real. Frederick Langley. Possibly the first to be erased.

She held the photograph longer than she should have, trying to find some flicker of recognition in the printed eyes. But it was just ink and paper. Still, it felt like being watched.

She slid the file into her bag. It hadn't started with Harper. Or Mick. Or her. It had always been happening. Only now did it seem to want to be found. She didn't leave. Not yet. There had to be more. A beginning. A point where the fracture had first split the world apart.

She carefully scanned the room again. Near the back, half-hidden behind a stack of disused shelving, she found it. A narrow metal door with a plaque, its paint peeling: Restricted Records – Special Cases.

She crossed to it. Tried the handle. Locked. Of course. She moved quickly now, drawers opening and shutting in soft, quick jerks. Pencils, old rubber bands, envelopes stained with the seep of forgotten teacups. And then, buried behind a ledger from the seventies, a ring of small brass keys. Cold. Slightly oily.

One fit.

Inside, the air was different. Still. Not dead, but waiting. The room was narrow, no windows, no signs, just a few plain cabinets. She opened the nearest drawer. The files were thin. Lighter than they should have been. No names. No headlines. Just fragments.

Scrawled notes. Dates that didn't match any known year. Events that hadn't happened, or had, and were forgotten. She flipped faster, her hands shaking now. One page. A man erased from a family photograph. Another. A theatre performance that never ended, even after the audience left. They weren't cases. They were corrections. Adjustments.

She pushed deeper into the drawer, papers sliding under her fingertips until she found it. A single typed note, clipped to a fragile report with a scrawl inked hastily along the bottom: Blackpool, 1896. The first fracture. The day the upgraded Winter Gardens opened.

Her mouth went dry. That date. That place. A hundred years before Harper. Before Mick. Before her. She stared at the page until the words blurred.

Until she thought she could hear distant music, thin and ghostly, under the crackle of the failing lights above her. A waltz. Applause. Then silence. She slipped the note into her bag, closed the drawer with careful hands.

She locked the door behind her. Replaced the keys where she had found them. When she stepped outside, the streets of Blackpool were still sleeping, blind to what moved through them. But Alice knew. She wasn't just following Harper's trail anymore. She was going to the source. To the beginning.

To the moment the world had first cracked and let something else through. And if the past was still there, still breathing beneath the pavements and the sea mist, then maybe the ones who had been taken weren't entirely gone. Maybe they were still waiting. Just beyond the edge of things.

Chapter 33

Alice had no illusions left about what she was doing. She wasn't retracing Harper Ross's steps anymore. That part, copying routes, cross-referencing dates, playing detective, had ended. Now, she was moving deeper. Following something older and quieter than any record could capture.

The Winter Gardens loomed ahead, the building picked out in weak pools of sodium light. Behind her, the town was hushed, the streets empty, the sea just a thin breath against the stones. A place like this didn't announce itself. It waited. It had always waited.

In 1896, something had shifted inside that building. Not broken. Not destroyed. Altered. Nudged off course just enough that the world, for all its stubbornness, couldn't quite put itself back. It hadn't stopped. It had kept working, quietly, like a leak spreading beneath wallpaper.

More than a century later, it still hadn't stopped.

She pulled her coat tighter around her and crossed the deserted square. Her boots made a soft, careful sound on the cold pavement, and her breath rose in pale clouds that vanished almost as soon as they formed.

The glass dome above the entrance caught the dull orange light and threw it back faintly, like a reflection smeared on old water. The doors stood closed but not forbidding. She reached for the handle. Paused. It wasn't fear. She had passed fear a long time ago. It was something else.

A quiet understanding. That she might not be the same on the other side. That there might not even be another side at all. She pushed.

The door opened too easily. No creak. No protest. Just the soft sweep of brass against wood and a sigh of air that felt wrong. Not stale. Not musty. Wrong, in the way a room feels wrong when you wake and realise you don't know where you are. She stepped inside. The door closed behind her without a sound. No echo. Only stillness.

The entrance hall stretched wide and hollow. The chandeliers overhead, once proud and glittering, hung like forgotten jewellery, frozen in mid-sway. Her footsteps rang out across the marble floor, too loud, too sharp. The whole building felt as if it were listening.

She took out her notebook and read in half-light.

On the last page, Harper's neat hand leaned sideways, almost whispering.

It doesn't want to be seen.

Alice read it once. Twice. Then clicked on her phone torch and moved forward. She passed the ticket booths first, their glass dusty and cracked, their frames peeling.

She didn't stop. She already knew where she was going: the oldest part of the Winter Gardens, buried behind everything newer, heavier, louder. A service door, warped by years of damp and neglect, hung slightly ajar. The air leaking through was thicker somehow. Still. No smell. No dust. Just a blank weight, like stepping into a photograph.

She pushed the door wider and entered the old auditorium. Rows of seats stretched away from her, perfect in their stillness, as if waiting for a sermon that had never come. The walls absorbed sound. Even the beam of her torch felt quieter here, thinner. She swept the light across the room: the fittings were intact. The curtains drawn back. The stage untouched.

And yet, something was wrong. It took her a moment to see it. A thin line across the stage floor centre, just visible in the angled light. She moved closer. At first it looked like a crack. Some old damage, left to fester.

But no. It was too clean. Too deliberate. A seam. As if the floor had been stitched together. As if the stage was hiding something behind a closed mouth.

She knelt carefully, the boards cold against her palms. Her fingers hovered over the seam. There was a shimmer there. Faint. Like heat above tarmac, though the air was cold. A wavering of texture. As if the wood itself was struggling to stay real.

Her throat tightened. She hesitated, one foot anchored to the boards, the other half-raised. The world behind her, the pub, the seafront, the thinning town, whispered through her memory like smoke, calling her back. But the fracture ahead breathed too, patient, and ancient, and it wasn't offering a second invitation. Slowly, deliberately, she touched it.

The shift was immediate. The floor gave a low groan, not a sound, exactly, more a shift in pressure, like a room flexing around a heartbeat. She stumbled back. The air turned, grew heavier. And then it appeared. Not a door. Not wood or glass or anything built by hand.

A tear in the air itself. Jagged at the edges, pulsing faintly, as if breathing. She stared at it. Her mind tried to place it as a mirror or a trick of the light, but no explanation came. It simply was. A black threshold cut into nothing.

She took out the notebook again, turned to a blank page. Her pen scratched across it, the sound almost invisible under the weight of the silence.

If I don't come back, I went through the first fracture. Find me.

She slipped the notebook back into her pocket. Stepped forward. Placed her hand on the edge of the opening. It wasn't cold. It wasn't warm. It had no temperature at all.

Chapter 34

Alice's breath came shallow and fast. Something was wrong with the theatre. It had the same high ceilings, the same heavy velvet curtains, but the chandeliers, once ornate and dazzling, now glowed with a sickly light, too pale, as if filtered through wax paper. Their glow clung to dust and heat, soaking the air in a damp, uneasy haze. The room smelled faintly of old perfume and something burnt, a scent long since extinguished but never entirely forgotten.

The seats were full, yet no one moved. What sat there weren't people in any recognisable sense but silhouettes, impressions that shimmered faintly, blurred at the edges as if drawn in smoke. Some were frozen mid-clap, others leaning forward, their features slack and indistinct, as though whatever had animated them had long slipped away. They weren't present. They were memory, residue left behind by whatever had come after.

At the centre of the stage stood Harper Ross. She hadn't changed. She didn't move. Her presence was solid, unmoving, as if she were a stone sunk into the middle of a still pond. Her eyes locked onto Alice's with that old intensity, but there was no flicker of recognition, no warmth, only something fixed, something that watched without blinking.

"You shouldn't be here," Harper said. The words cut through the heavy air, the kind of voice that belonged more to the building itself than the figure standing there.

Alice swallowed hard and took a cautious step forward, the floorboards beneath her boots creaking softly in the oppressive hush. "Neither should you," she said, her voice sounding too thin, too human for a place like this.

Harper didn't respond. She remained unnervingly still, as though placed there by a hand that had long since forgotten her. The theatre seemed to pulse, slow and heavy, the atmosphere growing denser with every second. Alice gripped her notebook tighter, though she could no longer remember what she had written in it. She steadied herself. "You were right," she said. "The Winter Gardens. The shifts. It started here, didn't it?"

Harper's jaw tensed, but she said nothing. Alice pressed on, forcing herself closer. "You left messages. Someone was meant to find them."

Harper tilted her head, a slight movement, almost mechanical. Her gaze didn't waver. "I didn't leave them for you." The words fell between them with the weight of finality. Alice's heart knocked against her ribs. So someone else had been expected. Or maybe it hadn't mattered who came, only that someone would.

She moved closer, slow, deliberate, as though wading through deep water. "Then tell me what this place is. What happened here?"

Harper hesitated, then exhaled a slow, strained breath, as if the act of speaking itself exacted a price. "This theatre was built in 1896. That much you already know." Alice nodded. "But it wasn't the first," Harper continued. "There was another theatre here before. Smaller. Humble. It burned down in 1895. No official cause. No survivors."

A tightness pulled in Alice's stomach. That wasn't in any of the records. She had combed through archives, read every missing persons report, every fire brigade log. There had been no mention of a fire. No hint that anything had stood here before. It hadn't been hidden. It had been removed.

Harper's voice remained steady, but there was a brittleness under it now. "It should have ended then. But the town wanted something grander. They rebuilt. Spared no expense. And the moment the doors opened again..." Harper's gaze shifted toward the audience.

Alice followed it. In the front row, one of the shadowed figures wore a bowler hat, tilted at an angle too precise to be natural. Beneath it, a frozen half-smile, the kind that broke when interrupted. Around it, the others leaned forward, utterly still. Silent. Watching.

"They let something in," Harper said quietly. Alice felt the words settle against her chest like a weight. The air thickened. The audience's attention, if it could be called that, turned toward them. Not with malice. Not with curiosity. Simply with inevitability. "Something came through," Harper said. "Something that didn't belong here. And it didn't just take people. It took context. It took time. It took everything that made sense."

Alice's mouth opened, but no words came. "It took history," she said finally.

Harper nodded once. "That's why the shifts happen. This isn't just forgetting. It's redacting. Rewriting. The world sealing over its wounds."

Alice thought of the pub, of the names that slipped away mid-conversation, of the blank spaces where faces used to be. It had never been about the missing. It had been about making the absences invisible.

"How do you know this?" she asked.

Harper ran a hand through her short hair, her fingers trembling slightly, as if trying to catch something just out of reach. "Because I was the last one who tried to stop it."

The silence that followed wasn't just absence of sound. It was thick. Heavy. As though the theatre itself had closed its eyes. "You're not the first, Alice," Harper said. "Mick wasn't. I wasn't. There were others before us. And if you stay, you won't be the last."

Alice's pulse raced, her breathing quick and shallow. "You think I don't know that?" she said. "You think I haven't seen what this place does to people?"

Harper's gaze sharpened, the faintest shadow of regret there. "You think you've seen something. You haven't. Not yet."

Alice stepped closer, the air tightening around her like wet cloth. "Then tell me. Help me understand."

Harper's mouth twitched, but she shook her head. "You still believe this is a puzzle. Something you can solve. You think if you dig deep enough, you'll find the root." She smiled then, not cruelly, not kindly, just sadly. "But this thing doesn't have a root. It has rot. It spreads."

Alice's hands clenched at her sides. "Then cut it out," she said.

Harper laughed, short and brittle. "You think I didn't try? I tried everything. I held on. I refused to forget. But the more you resist, the more it notices. The more it erases. Your name. Your reflection. Your place in time."

Her voice dropped, a confession. "That's how I ended up here."

The words hit Alice harder than she'd expected. "You're trapped."

Harper didn't deny it. She just looked tired.

"And if you keep pushing," Harper said, "you'll get trapped too."

Alice felt the rage rising, not at Harper, but at the hidden mechanism that allowed this to exist. "Then let's break it."

Harper's expression didn't change, but her voice softened. "You don't break this. You delay it. That's all. You hold it off a little longer than the one before you."

Alice looked into her eyes, steady, certain. "Then help me do that."

There was a long pause. Harper watching her. Weighing something. Finally, Harper stepped closer. "There might be a way."

The air seemed to draw tighter around them.

"Tell me," Alice whispered.

"You have to go back to the first night," Harper said.

Alice blinked, already knowing what she meant. "The fire."

Harper didn't flinch. "You have to go back to 1895."

Alice's mind scrambled for logic, for sense, but none came. And then, from behind her, she heard it. A chair scraped. Then another. The figures in the audience were no longer frozen. They rose one by one, their forms sharpening. Their silence thickening. The chandeliers above began to dim.

Harper's voice dropped, urgent now. "They know we're talking."

Alice turned. The audience was shifting, moving toward them.

Harper seized her wrist. "You don't have much time."

"Then tell me how!" Alice said, her voice breaking.

Harper's grip tightened painfully. "You already know how."

Alice caught a glimpse of something in her face, fear maybe, or sorrow, before the lights went out and the floor gave way beneath her. She fell into the dark, breathless, and the theatre let her go.

Chapter 35

Alice hit the ground hard. The world didn't catch her; it remade itself beneath her. The impact rattled through her bones, knocking the breath from her chest, leaving her stunned, belly-down against a surface slick and cold. For a moment, everything narrowed, light, sound, the quick thud of her heart hammering against her ribs. Her lungs seized for air, but when she finally managed to push herself upright, her hands sank slightly into wet cobblestones, her palms coated with grime. The light around her wasn't dim. It was piercing. Not electric. Not fluorescent. Gaslight. It shimmered against the smoke that curled lazily through the narrow streets, clinging to everything it touched. She stayed where she was, crouched low, heart hammering against the wet stone, listening. No cars, no distant hum of electricity, no chatter of tourists spilling from the pubs. Only the soft metallic shudder of a tram passing unseen and a faint, rhythmic squeak, a sign swinging on rusty hinges. Everything else was stifled, wrapped in a heavy, expectant silence.

She smelled it before she saw it, damp wood, horse manure, the sharp, acrid tang of burning coal. Somewhere nearby, a bell tolled, its tone flat and indifferent, joined by the steady murmur of voices. Not sharp or surprised, but casual, as if life had merely gone on uninterrupted. Her head still spinning, Alice blinked hard and raised her eyes. She was kneeling in the middle of a street, the stones uneven and slick with mud, water pooling in shallow hollows.

She couldn't tell if rain had fallen or was still falling. Her coat hung too heavily on her shoulders, rough wool that wasn't hers. Her boots pinched at the toes, unfamiliar.

She patted her pockets out of instinct. No phone. No notebook. No matchbook. The things that had tethered her, however thinly, were gone. She looked up, and the gas lamps lining the pavement threw out soft halos of golden light, blurring in the mist. People passed her by, men with stiff collars and hats, women whose skirts swept the ground, shoes squelching softly in the muck. A horse-drawn carriage rattled by close enough that muddy spray flecked the hem of her coat. The driver didn't even glance her way. No one did. The signs hanging from nearby buildings were hand-painted in curved, delicate lettering: Bootmaker, Stationer, Public House. Everything around her confirmed what she already knew in her bones.

She turned her head slowly, the unease rising inside her like a tide. And there it was. The Winter Gardens. Not as she had known it, but startlingly new. The brickwork sharp and clean, scaffolding clinging to the façade, men hammering and shouting above her. A half-built Ferris wheel loomed awkwardly nearby, its frame skeletal against the bruised sky. Buckets of turpentine and paint sat open along the kerb, the smell sharp enough to sting. She stared at the building, her throat dry, her hands trembling where they hovered uselessly at her sides. A newspaper rested on a bench near the theatre entrance, folded too neatly, almost posed. She moved toward it without thinking, but the closer she came, the more it seemed to blur, as if the ink refused to settle, as if the paper hadn't finished becoming real.

Alice pulled in a slow, bracing breath. It was 1895. She didn't need a date, didn't need to ask. The truth pressed in from every stone, every flicker of gaslight, every smell, every scuffed boot heel clicking past her. She had done it. She had crossed. And now she stood at the beginning, the first breach. The place where the world had cracked, letting something else through. And she had no idea how to get back.

She moved without deciding to, brushing at her coat as though she could scrub the grime away. Panic itched at the edges of her mind, but she forced it down.

There was no use in panicking. Not yet. She had a purpose. However tenuous. The fire. That was where it all began. If she could find it, understand it, maybe even prevent it, then perhaps she could unmake what was to come. She didn't know the rules here, but instinct warned her not to draw attention. She kept her head low, her pace steady, her face composed as she made her way toward the theatre.

The streets tightened around her. The air thickened with coal smoke and something acrid that clung to the back of her throat. The shops buzzed with quiet commerce, their signs swinging lightly on thin wires. A cart rattled past, crates marked Manchester stacked high, the driver muttering under his breath. Somewhere, a child cried and was quickly hushed. No one gave her a second look.

The newspaper shop sat at the end of a narrow lane, tucked against a fishmonger's whose prices smudged into illegibility on a damp chalkboard. Inside, the shop was tiny, the air smelled of ink and coal smoke. Broadsheets lined the shelves in careful, ordered stacks. Behind the counter stood a man with sleeves rolled to the elbow, his fingers stained blue with newsprint. He looked up slowly, his face unreadable, the look of a man who had spent too much time indoors.

Alice stepped forward, steadying her voice. "I'm looking for information," she said. "About the theatre."

He didn't blink. "You mean the Winter Gardens?"

She nodded once. "I heard there's been trouble."

He paused, his fingers tapping a slow, unconscious rhythm against the wood. "You're not the first to ask."

Her heart kicked hard against her ribs. "Who else?" she asked, keeping her tone even.

The man's eyes shifted, a subtle flicker. "A journalist. Langley. Frederick Langley." He studied her more closely now, suspicion threading into his voice. "You one of his lot?"

Alice met his gaze without flinching. "I just want to know what he found."

For a moment, it seemed he might refuse. But then he reached under the counter and pulled out a folded newspaper, the print still smudged at the edges.

She opened it carefully. The date at the top: September 23, 1895. Her eyes found the headline: Strange Occurrences at the Winter Gardens Construction Site.

Her fingers stiffened. The article spoke of shadows moving where there were no light sources, of doors appearing where no carpenter had planned them. It mentioned Langley by name, how he had taken an interest, how he had vowed to uncover the truth. The lines were strangely familiar, almost echoes of things she had read before. But they couldn't be. This was before any of it had begun.

She folded the paper slowly and looked up. "Where can I find him?"

The man shrugged, resigned. "Usually around the theatre, Miss. Poking around. Asking questions."

Alice murmured her thanks and stepped back into the street without looking back.

The light had shifted by the time she reached the Winter Gardens again. Dusk had settled in, clinging to the stones, turning everything a muted, bruised colour. The scaffolding threw long, twisted shadows. The workers were gone. The world had emptied itself, as if holding its breath.

She moved toward the entrance, her hands cold despite the thickness of her coat. The theatre stood before her, the first fracture point, waiting. The moment her foot crossed the threshold, something shifted. The noise of the street softened to a faint, muffled hum, like sounds underwater. The air grew thick and unmoving.

Inside, the theatre was hollow. Plaster dust floated like ash in the dim light. Wooden beams jutted from the floor like broken ribs. And near the unfinished stage, half lost in the shadows, stood a man. He wore a long coat, hands buried deep in the pockets, shoulders hunched as though listening for something that hadn't yet happened.

Alice stepped forward. "Langley?"

Her voice didn't echo, though the room was cavernous. He turned slowly. His face was gaunt, unreadable. There was recognition there, or the ghost of it, followed by doubt, then a flicker of fear. His mouth opened slightly, the beginning of a word, but whatever he tried to say dissolved into nothing.

He stared at her, his brow furrowed, as though trying to place her across a distance he couldn't bridge. His mouth moved again, a small, broken sound emerging, but no clarity.

Alice didn't move, didn't even breathe. He was here. Still whole. The first man to disappear. The first piece pulled loose from the weave. And now, before the fracture took him too, she had to learn what he knew, while there was still time.

Chapter 36

Alice stepped forward slowly, her pulse drumming in her ears. Frederick Langley stood just inside the entrance of the Winter Gardens, a tall figure drawn sharp against the half-light, the collar of his dark coat turned up against a wind that wasn't there. His face was sharper and older than the photograph she had seen in the archive, though no less familiar. He looked like something fixed in time, definite, immovable. But he was breathing. And she had to reach him before the world remembered to forget him.

Langley's brow furrowed, his voice roughened by suspicion. "You're not my reporter."

Alice let her breath go in a slow, unsteady exhale. "No," she said, voice low. "But I know what you've been looking for." His gaze shifted behind her, scanning the empty street, the dull glow of the gaslights, the clouded sky above. Not looking for escape, just measuring the time he had left. Then he sighed, rubbing his temple with a motion that spoke of slow deterioration. "Come in," he murmured. "Quickly."

She stepped past the threshold, the air pressing close against her skin. The door swung shut behind them with a soft, definitive sound, sealing them into the hollow, waiting building.

The main hall stretched vast and empty, cold enough that the breath barely left her mouth. No workers remained. No hammering. No casual shouts. Only the sound of their own footsteps and the low, restless groan of beams settling far overhead.

Dust floated in the stagnant air. Scaffolding rose up the walls like ribs of a decayed beast. The shadows didn't stay still. They shifted slightly, restless as if disturbed by breath.

Langley walked ahead with a brisk, urgent stride. Alice followed, her hands twitching uselessly at her sides. She had been here before. But never like this. The Winter Gardens now breathed with a presence she could feel against her skin, a held breath, a thing aware of her.

He stopped near the incomplete stage and turned, the movement of his coat a faint, reluctant sigh. His expression had hardened, eyes sharp. "You know something," he said. "And you've come a long way to find me."

Alice nodded once. She met his gaze, steady, cautious. "My name is Alice Whittaker," she said. "I'm... a journalist. Like you." Langley's eyes narrowed, suspicion refusing to release him. She pressed on. "I've been tracking disappearances. Not missing-persons cases. People who vanish without leaving a trace. No memory. No record. As if the world itself sealed over them."

His jaw twitched, but he said nothing. She could see him weighing her words, checking them against some private knowledge. "And I know you've been looking into the same thing," she added. "This place. The workers. The reports."

Langley reached into his coat and drew out a battered notebook. For a breath, her heart stilled. It looked like hers. He flipped quickly through the pages, then turned the book toward her, holding it open. "Read."

She leaned closer. The handwriting was hurried, angular, a spidery urgency pressed into the paper.

It doesn't want to be seen. Doors where there were none. The theatre is waking up.

Her skin crawled. She had written those same words once, or thought she had. Now she wasn't so sure.

Langley snapped the notebook shut with a small, impatient sound. "They see things," he said. "The workers. Doors that weren't there before. Figures moving at the edge of the halls. People who don't belong."

Alice nodded tightly. "That's how it starts."

His eyes locked on hers, sharp and almost accusing. "You've seen this before?"

"I've seen where it leads," she said quietly.

Langley turned his face away, toward the black, cavernous maw of the stage. His voice dropped when he spoke again. "So have I."

Alice frowned, her chest tightening. "What do you mean?"

He rubbed both hands roughly across his face, a gesture of a man fighting weariness at the bone. When he looked at her again, his eyes were bloodshot, rimmed with something more than exhaustion. "There's something wrong with this place," he said. "Not neglect. Not decay. Something that doesn't belong in the world at all. And it's been here longer than the bricks."

Alice's fists clenched slowly at her sides. "The shifts," she murmured.

Langley nodded grimly. "I don't know what it is. But I know when it started."

She didn't breathe. The air between them grew heavier. Langley turned fully toward the stage, the darkness beyond it stretching wide and patient. His voice barely rose above a whisper. "It started the night of the fire."

Alice swallowed hard, trying to steady herself. "What really happened that night?"

For a long moment, Langley said nothing. The creaks of the scaffolding filled the silence. Then: "There was a private event."

She tilted her head slightly. "A performance?"

He shook his head slowly, his mouth thinning. "No. Nothing in the schedules. No posters. No flyers. But people saw them arrive, men in evening suits, women in gowns stepping out of carriages. No one knew their names." He paused, his voice a low rasp. "They came quietly. Without announcement. They just walked in. The doors closed behind them."

Alice felt a chill skitter along her arms, an instinctive warning. "And then?"

Langley looked upward, at the crisscross of beams and broken rooflines. "That was the last time anyone saw them."

"No one came out?" Her voice sounded too small in the empty space.

He shook his head. "The fire started after midnight. No alarms. No witnesses. By the time people noticed the smoke, it was already too late."

Alice's heartbeat thudded in her ears. "How many?"

Langley's voice, when it came, was stripped of anything but fact. "No bodies were ever found."

She froze. "Nothing?"

"Not one," he said. "No bones. No ash. No clothing." He stared at her then, his gaze dull with a knowledge too heavy to share. "That's the question I've been trying to answer."

Alice stared back. This was it. The first crack in the world. Not a fire. Not an accident. An erasure.

"I need to stop it," she said, forcing the words out.

Langley's head snapped up sharply. His expression darkened in an instant. "You can't."

"I have to."

He stepped toward her, urgent now. "You don't understand. The fire didn't come after."

She blinked, confused. "What?"

His voice dropped lower, almost to a breath. "It happened before this part of the gardens was built."

The ground seemed to tilt beneath her feet. She stood very still. A coldness coiled through the hollow of her chest. Before she could form a reply, the chandeliers above them flickered violently, the bulbs dimming in sickly pulses.

Langley drew in a hard breath. Alice turned sharply, her body alert. The theatre was changing. Dust curled in the air, but not as before; it spiralled upward, as though escaping. The scaffolding groaned under some unseen weight. The floor beneath her boots vibrated softly, a warning. Langley stepped back. His face had gone slack, blankness draining into him.

"Langley!" Alice shouted, reaching for him.

His eyes found hers again, but they were blurred, his presence dimming before her. His mouth moved slowly. "Alice," he said, his voice little more than a breath of air. "I think I've already been erased."

Her breath hitched, caught somewhere painful. She stared at him, helpless, as behind them, something moved. A slow, patient shifting. Not new. Not unexpected. Something that had been waiting all along.

Chapter 37

The theatre was shifting around them. Alice could feel it not just in the shiver of the boards beneath her feet, but in the pressure behind her eyes, in the faint, oppressive change in the air, like the breath before a storm. Above, the wooden beams moaned softly, long and low, the sound stretched taut like a held note. The lights flickered, not randomly, but with a heavy, deliberate rhythm, as if something vast and half-awake stirred above them. She turned toward Langley. His face had drained of colour, his jaw slightly slack, but he wasn't afraid. Not exactly. There was something else in his eyes. Recognition. He wasn't watching the theatre unravel, he was remembering it. He knew what this was. And worse, he knew what came next.

Alice reached out and seized his arm. "We have to move. Now." He didn't resist. His body followed, but he moved like someone who had already surrendered to an ending, whose story had been written before she arrived. There was a slowness to him, not hesitation but resignation, as if the outcome had long since been decided and she was the only one still pretending otherwise. She pulled him harder, her fingers aching with the effort, forcing him toward the doors. Behind them, the floor trembled, not with violence but with the long, slow roll of something ancient shifting beneath their feet. Her pulse slammed against her throat. They ran, but their steps echoed strangely, their rhythm warped, slightly delayed, as if the theatre around them had begun to break away from time itself.

At the entrance, Alice threw herself against the doors, her shoulder jarring painfully with the impact. Nothing. Again, harder. Still nothing. The doors were locked, not just barred but sealed.

Langley exhaled beside her, his breath shallow but resigned. "It's not going to let us leave." His voice was hollow, certain.

Alice turned on him sharply. "I refuse to believe that." But even as the words left her, her gaze darted around the room, desperate. There, a side door, half-hidden behind a drooping velvet drape, just visible in the guttering light. She grabbed his wrist. "This way."

They moved quickly, feet making no sound now, as if the building had swallowed noise along with light. The side door gave under her hand with a surprising ease, swinging open on silent hinges. For a breath, hope flared. And then she saw it. Not a corridor. Not freedom. A single door. Then another. Then another, and another beyond that. Dozens, hundreds, stretching into the dark, each door slightly open, revealing only more doors beyond. A passage folding inward on itself, endless and impossible, like angled mirrors. She froze. Couldn't move. Langley stepped up beside her, his breath slow and shallow. He stared at the endless hall, and his voice, when it came, was stripped of wonder or fear, just tired understanding. "This is what it does."

Alice turned to him. He wasn't alarmed. He wasn't even curious. He was subdued, as if standing before a memory so old that it no longer carried weight. His shoulders sagged slightly. His eyes were flat. "I told you," he said quietly, almost to himself. "I think I've already been erased."

Her hands shook as she grabbed his face, forcing him to meet her eyes. "No. You're still here."

His gaze flickered across her, warm for a moment. "For now," he said. No bitterness. Only exhaustion, the kind that runs deeper than blood. The kind that belongs to things no longer fully anchored to the world.

Alice steadied her breathing, forced herself to think. "You said the fire happened before this theatre was added to the Winter Gardens. Before all of this."

Langley gave a faint nod, slow and uncertain, like dredging a memory from waterlogged depths. "Then it's already in the past," she said, her voice firming. "Which means the only way out is through."

She turned from the endless corridor of doors, faced the stage. It seemed farther than it had a moment ago, slightly raised, subtly wrong, as if space itself had bent while she wasn't looking. Langley didn't move. She reached for his hand again. "Trust me." His fingers hovered in the air for a second, then closed around hers. Together, they stepped forward.

The air grew heavier with each step. The effort to move felt immense, like walking through water thickened by ash. The light dimmed, not at once, but in patches, as though sections of the theatre were being switched off in advance of their passing. From somewhere behind them, Alice heard movement, slow, deliberate. The audience, or what was left of it, was no longer seated. They were rising. Turning. Watching. Not with faces, but with a kind of weight. She didn't look at them. She couldn't. Her gaze locked on the faint glow ahead, on the stage where the boards had begun to shimmer, where the heat rose in steady pulses.

The wood beneath her boots grew warm. Not burning yet, but rising, waiting. Something was coming. She gripped Langley's hand tighter. "We're going to step into it," she said. He hesitated, a half-second of doubt, then nodded once. Together, they jumped.

It wasn't falling. It was absence. The stage dissolved beneath them. Then the theatre. Then the world itself.

The fire arrived sudden and total, without source or warning. The ceiling vanished. The walls crumbled into dust. The chandeliers disintegrated into a fine, glittering mist. Everything collapsed inward in a silence too complete to be real. But there was no pain. Only the strange, weightless sensation of being suspended not in space, but outside it.

Alice felt her body become almost insubstantial. Langley was still beside her, his grip firm but growing lighter. His figure shimmered, half-formed, as if even here he was being pulled away. And then the world snapped.

She hit the ground hard. Cold stone slammed into her hands and knees. Air rushed into her lungs like water. The smell struck her next: soot, wet smoke, the acrid tang of burning wood and damp cobblestones. She gasped, coughing hard, the noise raw against the night.

Around her, darkness pressed in, thick and low. But behind her was an orange glow. Rising. Consuming. The Winter Gardens was on fire. Not a vision. Not a memory. The fire. The real one.

People screamed. Buckets passed hand to hand in frantic chains. Someone shouted for help. Another voice rose in prayer. The heat, the panic, the urgency belonged to the living, not the dead.

Alice turned sharply. Langley knelt nearby, dazed. His eyes blinked slowly, unfocused. "Langley," she gasped, staggering to him. "We're in the past. The fire is happening now." He didn't answer. She shook him hard by the shoulders. "Do you hear me? We made it!"

He turned toward her. But his eyes floated strangely. Pale, too wide. Detached. His body was here, but his presence, the thing that made him Langley, was slipping.

She felt it before he said it. "I was never supposed to leave," he murmured. The words cut like a blade drawn slow and deep.

"No." She shook her head, violently now. "You're here. You're still here."

Langley's lips barely moved. "I don't think I'm real anymore."

She grabbed his coat, clung to it, the fabric soaked with rain and smoke. "You are. You have to be."

He looked at her properly then, for the last time, and smiled. Not with triumph. Not with sadness. With recognition. "Alice," he said softly. "You made it."

And then he was gone. His outline blurred, softened, then scattered like smoke torn loose from the fire.

Alice was left kneeling alone on the cold stone, the fire raging behind her, the old town echoing with human panic. Voices rose and fell. Buckets slammed into stone. And somewhere, hidden deep beneath the smoke, the ash, the roar of the flames, the cycle waited. Waiting to begin again.

Chapter 38

The Winter Gardens burned before her. Not in the way buildings normally did, not in panicked spurts or collapsing groans, but with a strange deliberateness, as if the fire had remembered something. Flames climbed the skeletal ironwork of the unfinished theatre, curling around the exposed beams with desperate, inevitable hunger. Smoke coiled into the sky, thick and indifferent, painting the night above Blackpool in streaks of orange and grey. The air tasted scorched, metallic, bitter against the back of her tongue. Alice stood still in the middle of the street, breath coming in short, hot gasps. The cobbles beneath her feet were slick from the earlier rain, reflecting the flickering light in broken, scattered patterns. Somewhere, a bell tolled, distant, dulled by the heavy smoke. Life, or the brittle shape of it, still moved through the town, but something had come loose beneath the surface, slipping out of step.

Langley was gone. She didn't know when. There had been no sound, no flash, no warning. Just a hollowing out, a sense that something essential had simply ceased to be. Behind her, people ran in and out of view, shouting names, barking orders, muttering prayers. Someone, the mayor maybe, Frederick, something, stood red-faced at the entrance, waving people forward with a handkerchief clenched in one sweaty fist. Labourers dragged beams away from the doors, others stumbled back from the smoke empty-handed. But it was all background noise to Alice now. Unimportant. She already knew what they didn't. That this fire wasn't natural. That it wasn't really a fire at all.

Her mind moved quickly, though not in a straight line. She thought of the missing records, the blank spaces in the archives, the way no cause had ever been found, no bodies recovered. It had been recorded as a fire because the world needed something simple. But that wasn't what had happened. It wasn't death. It wasn't survival. It was something else. As if everyone inside had simply stopped being. As if erased. And now, she was here, standing at the edge of that moment, watching it unfold in real time. The first shift. The first fracture in reality. And she had minutes, maybe less.

She turned without thinking, scanning the confusion around her, looking for an opening. Labourers moved like figures in a dream, frantic but unfocused. A child clung to a lamp-post, screaming. The mayor's chain glinted in the firelight as he barked at the bucket chain. None of it mattered. Water couldn't extinguish something that hadn't truly ignited. This wasn't combustion. It was ritual. It was invitation. And the source of it was still inside.

Alice ran, ducking past a man sloshing a pail, weaving through the smoke. Her coat clung wetly to her legs. The heat struck her in waves, first as a warning, then as punishment. Inside, the walls groaned and hissed, wood surrendering slowly to silence. Each step dragged at her, heavier than the last. The air stung her eyes, burned her throat, but she kept moving. She didn't think. She didn't hesitate. She simply followed something older and more urgent than reason. And then she saw them.

The flames weren't spreading naturally. They thickened around the stage, swirling inward, drawn to a centre point. Five figures stood there, unmoving, untouched by the fire's heat. Their faces were blurred by smoke, their robes clinging to their bodies like shadows. They weren't panicked. They hadn't rushed inside to save anyone. They had been waiting. Maybe they had always been here. Alice slowed, her chest tightening, not just from the smoke but from the weight of recognition. She didn't know them. And yet she understood them. This wasn't an accident. The theatre hadn't simply caught fire. It had been offered. A ritual was underway.

She moved closer, her boots crunching over broken glass and splintered wood. The five figures formed an uneven ring around something she couldn't work out. Next to it was an old high-back chair. Empty. Not an absence but a space being held. Reserved. The air thickened, pressing at her temples, blurring the edges of her vision. This was the beginning. The fractures. The disappearances. The wrongness that would ripple out through the years. Whoever they were, they had invited it in. That was enough. She didn't need to know their names.

Alice's gaze darted upward. The roof groaned under the strain, the bones of the theatre sagging with heat. Above the stage, a support beam, already scorched and cracking, hung at a dangerous angle, its joints shrieking quietly. She scanned the floor. Found a length of timber, burning at one end. Without thinking, she grabbed it. Pain lanced through her palms, but she didn't let go. There wasn't time. She swung the plank hard against the base of the support beam. The sound it made was dull, tired. The robed figures didn't move. She swung again. Harder.

This time, something gave.

The beam split with a sharp, wet crack, like the snapping of the world's spine. It fell. The stage broke open, a spray of sparks and splinters. The five figures scattered silently, without a sound of fear, without any sound at all. The fire roared in sudden protest, rising, angry, alive. Alice staggered backwards as the ground beneath her buckled slightly, a great breath sucked inward. For a terrible second, she thought she had made it worse.

The heat surged around her. The walls bent inward under invisible pressure. And then, slowly, it began to recede. Not all at once. Not cleanly. But like the tide pulling back, sluggish, and reluctant. The wrongness lifted. The shift, whatever it had been, recoiled. The fire still burned, viciously, hungrily, but now it was just fire. Brutal, real. The kind that left ash behind. Not void.

Alice let out a shaky breath. Her body ached from effort and from fear. Her hands throbbed where the skin had already begun to blister. But she had done it. She had stopped the fracture. The theatre would fall, but the world would hold.

She turned toward the doors, dragging one foot in front of the other. Smoke coiled around her, caught on her clothes, clawed at her throat. The doorway was close. But the fire had grown faster than she expected. Her lungs screamed. Her vision narrowed. She wasn't going to make it.

Then, fingers closed around her wrist, warm, solid. She gasped. Looked up. Langley. Or what was left of him. He shimmered faintly at the edges, as though the world still wasn't sure he belonged. But his grip was firm. Real. He pulled her forward, no words, no time. She stumbled after him.

Together, they broke through the smoking doorway into the cold night air.

Alice collapsed onto the cobbles, coughing so hard her ribs ached. Her palms were blistered and raw. Behind her, the Winter Gardens roared, flames licking hungrily at the sky. But the fracture was gone. The shift had passed. The town, the timeline, it held.

Langley stood over her, fading fast. His expression was calm, almost tender. She reached for him, but her hand passed through smoke. He didn't flinch. He only smiled faintly as if remembering something.

"You did it," he said.

She opened her mouth to answer, but the words caught. And then he was gone. Not pulled away. Not erased. Just... gone. As if a page had been turned, and he had simply never been printed on it at all.

Alice stayed there for a moment longer, listening to the chaos behind her: the clash of buckets, the rise and fall of voices. But none of it was strange anymore. No flickering time. No blank spaces where people should be. Just panic. Just life. Understandable. Human.

She rose slowly, every movement raw and painful. She reached into her coat pocket, not even sure why. Her fingers brushed something dry. Paper.

She pulled it out, unfolded it carefully. A small, browned scrap. Her breath caught.

Three words, scrawled in uneven ink.

Find the last.

She stared at them, unblinking. The last what? The last fracture? The last survivor? The last witness? She didn't know yet. But she folded the note carefully into her palm, feeling its rough corners press against her skin. Then, with the Winter Gardens burning and the town blissfully unaware of what had almost unravelled, Alice turned away from the fire.

Chapter 39

Alice stayed near the fire, her shoulders slightly hunched, fingers tightening around the folded note. Smoke slid past her cheeks, moving with a strange deliberateness, its heat blunted by the cold damp of the Blackpool night. The note had softened with sweat, ink smudging faintly, but the message echoed in her mind. *Find the last.* The words didn't press with urgency; they weighed, slow and inevitable, like a memory just surfacing. She had stopped the shift. The fire, whatever it had meant, was nearly over. But she was still here, drawn tight into a year that wasn't hers, 1895 pressing around her with a strange permanence. Behind her, the Winter Gardens groaned as if in mourning, flames leaping within the ribcage of its rafters. Across the square, people shouted, moving like marionettes in smoke, the rhythm broken and frantic. Someone yelled for water. Another voice answered, too distant to help.

She turned slowly, letting her eyes move across the chaos. The mayor's hat had been lost, his silver chain dulled with ash. Workers stumbled back and forth, their arms straining with buckets, sleeves soaked to the elbow. A group of children huddled beneath a boarded-up shopfront, eyes wide and blank, unmoving. Alice scanned the crowd again, slower this time, letting her gaze rest on each face a little too long, as if trying to recall names she had never learned. Something prickled at the back of her skull, not a thought, but a presence unaccounted for. She couldn't say what was missing, only that it was.

Then it came. The robed ones.

She had seen them. Hadn't she? Before the beam collapsed. Before the fire surged. They had scattered, but they hadn't run like the others. No. She couldn't remember them moving at all. It was like they had slipped between frames, bypassing panic, bypassing time itself. If they had begun the fracture, perhaps one of them remained. Still connected. Still unfinished. Her fingers tightened around the note, and without fully deciding to, she moved.

The lane to her left was thinner than she remembered, walls pressing in with the weight of damp stone and mildew. Her boots struck uneven cobbles slick with ash and rain, her breath quickening as she moved past crates, crates she somehow knew would be gone if she looked for them tomorrow. The crowd noise dulled behind her, replaced by her footsteps and the soft, muffled steps of another just ahead. A figure moved through the alley, their robes dark and clumsy, the shape of them human but hesitant, as if the act of walking was unfamiliar. Alice closed the gap carefully. The fire didn't reach here. The light faded into something older, and the air was thick with the smell of scorched wood, old coal smoke, and something else, something like wax or damp cloth long hidden.

The figure stumbled. A sound, half grunt, half sob. They went down hard, their robes tangling around them. Alice caught up in time to see them scrabbling against the stone, and without thinking, she reached out and grabbed their wrist. The flesh beneath was warm and human, the pulse fluttering fast. "Stop," she said, her voice hoarse but steady. The figure froze. She reached for the hood and pulled it back. The street dropped away from her, not literally, but in the way it does when something too strange becomes suddenly, undeniably real.

A young woman. Early twenties, maybe younger. Dark curls plastered to her face, mouth parted in panic, eyes wide with something deeper than fear. Alice stared at her, the rest of the alley forgotten. She knew this face. Not personally, but well enough. She had seen it in the archives, yellowed paper, grainy print, a photo pinned carelessly among the lost. One of the missing. One of the ones presumed burned in the fire. But not burned. Not lost. Found, now, in flesh and breath.

"You," Alice said, more to herself than to the girl.

The woman blinked rapidly, still dazed. "I... I don't understand. Who are you?" Her voice cracked, fragile.

Alice didn't answer. She had no name to give that would matter here. The note, soft now between her fingers, whispered again in her mind. *Find the last.* It wasn't an instruction anymore. It was recognition. This girl, this last one, had not vanished. She had escaped.

Alice pulled her gently into the shadows, away from the drifting, distracted witnesses. The bricks were slick with condensation, the smoke overhead moving in slow, indifferent sheets. "I need to know what happened inside the theatre," she said, her voice low, nearly a whisper.

The woman stiffened. Her hands shook, then curled in toward her body like something trying to hide. "I don't know," she said, but even she didn't sound convinced.

"You do," Alice said, softer. No accusation. Just fact.

The girl's lips moved, silent, shaping words she couldn't yet say. Then, slowly, her eyes glassed over, and she whispered, "I was supposed to go." The sentence hung between them, heavier than all the smoke.

Alice felt her stomach twist, low and cold. "Go where?" she asked, but the answer was already taking shape in her mind.

The woman's face changed. "They said it was a passage. A way to… step outside. To become more than this." Her voice faltered. It sounded rehearsed, like she was repeating someone else's promises.

Alice felt the cold creep deeper despite the heat rolling from the burning theatre. She had heard fragments of this before, phrases half-spoken, memory gaps where names should have been. The fire hadn't been a tragedy. It had been a door. Forced open. A fracture too deep for time to mend.

"But you didn't go," Alice said, already knowing.

The woman shook her head, tears streaking ash down her cheeks. "I got scared. I ran. Before the doors opened." Her voice tore on the last word, weak and thin as wet paper. Alice stood still, feeling the weight of it. The fracture hadn't killed these people. It had accepted them. All but one.

"Where?" Alice asked. "Where did you run?"

The woman wiped at her face, breath hitching. "Behind the theatre. The alley. I didn't think. I just went."

Alice nodded once. That alley still existed. In her own time, it was a dead end. But maybe time was the lie. Maybe dead ends weren't endings at all.

She stepped back, took the girl's hand briefly, then let it go. "You have to come with me," she said.

The woman only shook her head, a small, tired gesture. "I can't," she whispered. "I don't belong anywhere anymore." No anger. No self-pity. Just a simple, tired truth.

Alice understood. It was a sensation she knew too well. She let the young woman, walk away and then turned and moved toward the rear of the theatre. The smoke thickened. Crates had been knocked aside, ash scattered over the cobbles. The alley narrowed, and at its end loomed a blank brick wall, slick with damp. She slowed, her heart steady but her hands trembling, as if her body knew something her mind had not yet caught up to.

She reached the wall and let her hand hover close. There was nothing she could see. But she wasn't looking for something visible. She closed her eyes and waited. Her fingers twitched, brushing something cold, too smooth, too still. Not quite wall. Not quite air. A shimmer, like heat above tarmac, but wrong. The seam. The edge. The place where the world thinned.

Alice drew a sharp, metallic breath, and stepped forward, into whatever came next.

Chapter 40

Alice fell forward with a gasp, her hands striking the pavement before her knees buckled. The ground was wet and gritty, the film of the streets clinging to her skin, salt from the sea, traces of petrol, that faint stickiness of rain mixed with engine residue that never quite dried. She coughed, not hard but deep in the throat, as if her lungs were still somewhere between two worlds. The air was familiar, heavy with the wrong season. Above her, a streetlamp buzzed with the dull rattle of a failing bulb. Beyond it, the sounds of traffic murmured, a lorry changing gears, the faint bark of a horn, wheels hissing through puddles. Somewhere in the distance, a gull gave a thin cry, quickly swallowed by the night.

She sat back on her heels, blinking against the sharp neon wash from a nearby shopfront. Her chest heaved, not from exertion but from recognition. She was back. She was in Blackpool. Or what should have been Blackpool. But something was wrong. The air smelled the same. The pavement bore the same old mix of concrete, chewing gum, and oil stains. Yet her skin prickled. There was a detail out of place, and she didn't know what it was yet. Only that it was waiting. Her hand brushed against something on the ground, a charred matchbook, its lettering half-erased. It bore no name she recognised, only the outline of a theatre she once knew. She closed her fingers around it, a small weight anchoring her to this version of Blackpool, whatever it had become.

She stood slowly, brushing her coat with hands that still trembled. The street was one she knew.

A narrow back lane near the promenade, where the curve of the buildings funnelled the sea breeze into a constant whisper. The Seagull's Rest would be just around the bend. Hopefully, that, at least, hadn't changed. She checked her pockets, her phone was there. Her notebook, too. She pulled it out and opened it to the last page, where her own handwriting stared back at her, scratched and rushed: *Find the last.* But beneath it, something new. A second line. The pen strokes thicker, the words unfamiliar.

You weren't supposed to make it.

Her throat tightened. The words sat too neatly on the page as if they had been waiting for her to read them. She closed the book without thinking, the snap of the pages echoing too loud against the quiet brick. She shoved it into her coat and stepped toward the main road.

She was halfway across the street before she stopped. Her breath caught, not from fear, but from the sudden awareness of something gone. Across from her, where Baxter & Co. had stood for as long as she could remember, where she had bought her coat the previous winter, where the bell above the door had jingled with that old-fashioned sound, there was nothing. No windows. No signage. No boarded-up facade or closing-down notice. Just a wall. Flat, clean brick. Seamless. As if the shop had never existed. She stepped closer, half-expecting to see some trace, a ghost of a sign, a rusted bracket, the outline of a door lost beneath a new coat of paint. But there was nothing. It wasn't a change. It was an erasure. She stood in the middle of the road, as if by standing still, the shape of the past might somehow reappear.

She walked on, boots ticking against the kerb. The cold had deepened now, or perhaps she had simply started to feel it again. The Seagull's Rest came into view, its familiar yellow light spilling across the pavement. She pushed the door open and was hit at once by the old mix of beer, vinegar, and fried food, so strong it clung to the throat, a smell that lived in the walls.

The pub looked the same. Sheila was behind the bar, sleeves rolled, and her hair tied up in that loose, practical knot. The hum of voices, the soft creak of wooden stools, the jukebox humming something low and familiar. She let the warmth settle into her skin. It was almost a comfort.

But not entirely.

She scanned the room without meaning to, her eyes flicking from face to face. Most were as they had been. Regulars in their usual places. But not all. A man who had always sat in the corner, near the fruit machine, a quiet man, Jack something, who muttered at the crossword and ordered small glasses of bitter, was gone. In his place sat someone younger, smoother, dressed in a clean navy coat, sipping clear gin without ice. She walked to the bar, her voice quiet. "Sheila,"

The landlady looked up, nodding as if nothing were strange. "Alright, love?"

Alice gestured slightly toward the corner. "The man who used to sit there. What was his name again?"

Sheila frowned, not dismissively, but as if the question made no sense. "No one sits there regular. That lad's been coming in a few weeks now."

Alice said nothing. Just turned back, staring at the man who had replaced someone. Or something. He didn't look at her. He kept sipping his drink as though he belonged to this place and always had. She stepped away slowly, her breath suddenly sharp in her chest.

It wasn't just him. There were other absences. Small ones. Some people were fixed in place, exactly where they belonged. But others… others had been moved, or erased. Like tiles in a mosaic, lifted and replaced, the shape intact, but the pattern changed. The shift had stopped. She was sure of that. But it hadn't stopped cleanly. The seams were still visible if you knew where to look.

She left the pub without speaking, the warmth behind her fading quickly in the damp air. The wind off the sea caught her coat, tugging gently. She walked fast, past closed shutters and uneven pavements, until she reached the newsstand near the tram line.

It was still open, the same old man behind the counter, though he didn't meet her eyes. She handed over a coin, took the day's edition of The Blackpool Chronicle, and unfolded it beneath the glow of the flickering streetlamp. The paper was damp around the edges, the ink slightly smudged.

She skimmed quickly. Local council disputes. A reopened case about stolen copper wiring. Then, lower on the front page, a piece that shouldn't have been there. Local Journalist Found Dead in North Pier Alleyway. She reread the headline, then the short paragraph beneath.

The body of a local writer was discovered late last night in an alley near North Pier. Authorities say there were no signs of foul play, but the exact circumstances remain unclear. The individual, who had no known family or close acquaintances, is believed to have suffered a sudden cardiac episode.

No name. No photograph. Just a vague outline of a life, erased before anyone had reason to ask why.

Her fingers clenched around the paper. She didn't need a name. She knew. It was her. Not this her, not the one who stood here reading the report under a broken light. The other version. The one who hadn't come back. The one who had been left behind or replaced. The world had written her out cleanly, almost kindly. An unnamed death. A tidy explanation.

She folded the paper, tucked it into her coat, and looked down the street. The buildings stood in silence. The wind stirred the edges of an abandoned crisp packet. A bus turned the corner without stopping. She didn't move.

She had made it back. That much was true. But the rules had shifted in the doing. Something watched. Something knew. And the game was still going on somewhere in the town, behind these false fronts and overwritten names.

Chapter 41

Alice stood beneath the dim halo of a flickering streetlamp, the mist curling around her boots and the folded newspaper pressing heavily against her hip. Blackpool was too quiet, perhaps, but not in any way that would alarm the passers-by drifting home from late buses or the nightclubs. To them, everything looked just as it should: the pub still glowing on the corner, the pavement slick with rain, the street signs still pointing the way home. But Alice knew. The shift hadn't undone her. She had survived. Rewritten the script, torn the page and replaced it with another. Yet the stitching hadn't held. Something in the world still resisted her presence, and she felt it watching, lurking in the spaces between shopfronts that shouldn't be there, in the flickers of doubt across faces that ought to have known her. The Winter Gardens had burned in 1895, and no fractures had opened then. That should have been enough. But the obituary with no name said otherwise. A version of her, the version that should have been erased, had remained. Or worse, had returned.

She walked. Past the fish bar with its metal shutters pulled halfway down, past the shop that had sold newspapers since she was a child, except now it didn't exist. In its place stood a flat-faced unit with 'TO LET' in bold red lettering.

The rhythm of the town was wrong; it was out of step, like a record played just slightly too slow. Long since demolished, the post office stood now with its old brickwork intact, its letterbox painted over but still bearing the Royal insignia.

Sheila still ran the pub, laughing too loudly through the open door. The Chronicle was still being printed, its presses grinding through the night, churning out births, deaths, council disputes. But none of it made sense. The surface held, but underneath, reality trembled. The town held its shape, but the pieces didn't fit, like a memory patched together by someone else's hand. She knew how this worked now. How the world corrected itself and nudged things back into alignment with soft, cruel pressure. If she waited too long, it would choose its own way of doing so.

The Chronicle office hadn't changed in years, a plain building with rattling windows and tired lights that made everything inside look jaundiced. She paused across the road, squinting past the glass. And there, in her old place, her desk, her chipped mug, her login details taped to the side of the monitor, sat herself. Not a ghost. Not a memory. Alice Whittaker, the version that had existed before all this, typing as though the world hadn't shuddered sideways. Her stomach tightened, a slow knot forming behind her ribs. It wasn't just that her life had gone on without her. It had split. The shift hadn't erased her; it had duplicated her. And now there were two Alices, impossibly alike, impossibly wrong. The world wouldn't tolerate that for long. It wasn't a matter of who deserved to stay. It was a question of symmetry, of balance. Which version would be allowed to remain?

She turned sharply and walked. The cold had settled into her collarbone. She crossed the promenade, boots clapping against the slick paving stones, heading for the place where the fracture had once begun, an alley behind the Winter Gardens, half-forgotten, easy to overlook. The sort of place the world wouldn't miss if it vanished. The air grew heavier, saturated with brine and something metallic and old. A crate sat overturned near the wall, spilling sodden wrappers and a plastic fork. The bin beside it had split open, leaking a slow stain into the gutter.

She crouched, withdrawing the newspaper again, unfolding it with shaking fingers. The obituary was still there. Vague, incomplete. "No signs of foul play. Details remain unclear."

No name. No date. Just absence. Not a death, but a deletion. She pressed her palm against the cold concrete and held it there, eyes closed. The world here was thinner, threadbare, a memory that reality had tried to expunge but hadn't quite managed.

Something shifted. Not a sound, just the air changing weight. She opened her eyes, scanning the alley. No one. But the quiet had deepened. A stillness had taken hold. She reached out, not with her hand, but with something older, more instinctive, the same way she had in 1895 when the fracture had opened and everything she knew had been doubted. Again, she felt it. A subtle give in the air, a soft seam between worlds. Without hesitation, she stepped forward.

It happened gently. The light stilled. The alley remained the same in shape and form, but its atmosphere shifted, grew muffled. The buzzing of the streetlamps dimmed. The town beyond faded into a grey hush. And there, against the far wall, stood another Alice. Her coat. Her face. Her posture. All mirrored exactly. But the eyes, there was nothing in them. Not dead. Not hostile. Just... absent. She was like a figure in a photograph, waiting for the shutter to close. Alice approached slowly, unsure whether to speak. The other looked up.

"You shouldn't be here," she said. The voice was flat, matter-of-fact.

Alice's mouth was dry. "That makes two of us."

"There can't be two," the other continued, head tilting slightly as if confirming the weight of her own words.

"I know," Alice said quietly.

They were silent then, the two of them facing each other in the liminal hush of a reality stretched too thin. Then the erased Alice smiled, not warmly, not cruelly, just the faintest curl of the lips. And Alice understood.

It had never been about which of them deserved to stay. The fracture hadn't failed. It had hesitated. The world wasn't waiting to correct itself.

It was waiting for her to choose. She stepped forward, reaching out her hand. The other did the same. When their fingers touched, there was no explosion, no light. Only stillness. A feeling of deep, silent recalibration.

She stumbled. Air rushed back into her lungs. The alley was back to normal, solid and detailed. A taxi passed nearby, its tyres hissing through a puddle. The stink of seaweed and chip wrappers returned. The town had remembered itself. She turned slowly, half-expecting something still to be wrong. But the post office was gone again. The shops were where they should be. People walked past without pause. She reached into her coat pocket. The obituary was gone. In its place, the notebook she had always carried. On its last page, a message had appeared in her own scrawl.

You were supposed to be here.

She stood for a moment longer, listening. Then, without another glance at the alley, she stepped onto the pavement and walked back into a world that had finally, quietly, allowed her to remain.

Chapter 42

Blackpool at night smelled of the sea and fast food, the pavement still tacky from the remnants of the day's crowd. The arcades had long since shut, their neon signs humming into silence, and the air was damp, heavier than mist, not quite rain, clinging to her skin. Alice moved through it with the careful step of someone returning to a place that vaguely remembered her. She was here. She was real. And for the first time since the fire in 1895, since the theatre had cracked open and time had folded in on itself, she felt a sort of stillness. Not triumph, not even relief, just an ending. The world hadn't shattered. She hadn't disappeared. But neither had it gone back to what it had been. Something had settled, but it hadn't settled cleanly.

She reached the edge of North Pier and paused with one hand on the railing, its iron slick with salt and age. The black and featureless sea stretched ahead of her, breathing in long, indifferent waves. There were no stars, only the faint suggestion of light far offshore. She stood there a while, listening to the sea's hush and the creak of the structure beneath her feet. Her breath came slow, measured. She had spent days, weeks, maybe longer, fighting to hold onto this reality, to keep her footing when everything shifted beneath it. And now that she had it, now that she was standing on solid ground again, she found herself unsure of what to do with it.

She took her notebook from her coat pocket. The cover was worn soft at the corners, the pages swollen slightly from damp. She flipped it open with numb fingers. The last message was still there: *You were supposed to be here.*

It hadn't faded. The ink held. And so did she. She had made it through, somehow. Merged with the part of herself that had been excised. Closed the loop. Stopped the shift, though that word felt flimsy now, barely containing what had happened. But even so, the question lingered, quiet and persistent: was it truly over?

Her thoughts moved without her bidding. Mick had seen the cracks, but too late to outrun them. Harper, caught in the fold, repeating the same hour until her voice wore thin. Langley, calm and still amid the burning seats of the theatre, as if he had always known he wouldn't be walking out. All of them had slipped away. And she had remained. Not out of brilliance. Not out of courage. Simply because she hadn't let go. She had refused. That was all. And that refusal had somehow mattered more than anything else.

She let out a breath, slow and shallow, as if exhaling too sharply might start something moving again. The town looked normal now. Clean edges. Stable colours. People walked the streets again with purpose, not the soft, disoriented drift of those caught between realities. But she remembered. She remembered the way the streetlights had doubled, how shadows had stretched too far, how time had folded like a map no one had known how to read. The world had cracked and corrected itself. Buildings had returned. Names had settled back into place. But Alice still carried the memory of the fracture. And no one else seemed to notice. The world hadn't paused for her. No one at the Chronicle had asked where she'd been. Her neighbours passed her with the same absent nods. The man at the corner shop didn't even blink. That was the part she couldn't quite absorb, not the terror, not the burning, not the unmaking of reality, but the indifference. The way life went on as though she had never left it.

She turned away from the sea and walked back into town. Her shoes scuffed softly against the wet pavement. The occasional taxi idled near the kerb, headlights painting the buildings in flickers of white. The shops had all returned. Their signs glowed dully in the night.

No more echoing storefronts, no more duplicated signs, no more faces that blurred at the edges. It was all back to what it had been. Except her. She remembered everything. She remembered too much. The fracture hadn't taken her, but it had left its imprint, faint and lingering.

Mick's voice surfaced again in her mind, quiet, certain, already half-accepting of what was coming. Harper's laughter edged with something brittle. Langley's last look, unblinking as the fire reached his shoes. She had made it through. And that was the heaviest part. The solitude of survival. The guilt of being the one who returned when so many hadn't. The mind doesn't know how to carry absence. It just keeps turning it over, again and again, hoping the shape will change.

Her street remained the same. A single lamp pooled yellow light across the pavement. The door to her building stuck slightly, just as it always had. The takeaway menu was still wedged in the letterbox. It might have been yesterday. It might have been a hundred years ago. She climbed the stairs slowly, the bannister cool under her hand, the air thick with the scent of dust and old carpet. Her key turned in the lock, stiff but obedient. The flat opened to silence. Nothing had moved. The desk, the mug, the unwashed plate by the sink, they all waited as if time had held its breath in her absence.

She closed the door behind her, let her coat fall over the chair, and stepped into the hallway. And there, in the mirror, she saw it. Just for a second. A flicker. Her reflection. Only, it didn't blink. It looked at her. Watched. Then, in the next breath, it was gone. Everything was normal. Her own face, pale and drawn, staring back. Nothing out of place. Nothing wrong. And yet.

She stepped closer. Touched the frame. The mirror was cool, solid. Her reflection followed her movements precisely. No delay. No distortion. But something had shifted inside her. A weight, a question. Had she really come back whole? Or had some part of her stayed behind, curled in the corner of that fractured space, watching from the dark?

Her body was beginning to ache, not from effort but from the long stretch of tension that had never quite eased. She stepped away from the mirror, moved to the bed, sat down carefully, as if her body might betray her if handled too quickly. She let herself lie back, arms folded across her chest, eyes tracing the lines of the ceiling. The room was quiet. The walls held firm. No warping, no flickering.

The world was holding. She was still here. And for tonight, that was enough. Almost. In the kitchen, the kettle clicked. She hadn't plugged it in.

Chapter 43

Alice woke to the faint rustle of paper, a gentle scraping that barely disturbed the stillness of the room. At first, she convinced herself it was just the wind slipping quietly through the gap in her window, brushing gently against loose papers, but then came another sound, softer, more deliberate. Her breath caught tight in her chest, and she sat up slowly, muscles rigid beneath her skin. The room was still shrouded in darkness, the earliest threads of dawn barely seeping through the heavy curtains. The flat around her was hushed, almost unnaturally quiet, yet it felt subtly changed. She turned her head carefully, the movement cautious and fearful, and froze at what she saw: a slip of paper lying quietly on the floor, just below the closed bedroom door. It hadn't been there before.

Alice's mouth went dry, a chill crawling across her skin. Slowly, she reached down, her fingers trembling as they brushed the thin, yellowed sheet. It felt fragile, aged by time it shouldn't yet have known. She hesitated, bracing herself before turning it over. Her pulse quickened unbearably, fingertips growing numb with dread as she struggled to steady her breath. Then, with a sinking feeling, she allowed herself to read the note. Three words were scrawled across it.

You left something.

Her breath hitched again, panic rising from a deeper place within, her stomach twisting sharply. She recognised that handwriting instantly, the slight slant, the hesitant curve. It was hers.

She flipped the note over, hoping desperately for clarity, but the reverse was blank, devoid of answers. The ink, faded and smudged, looked as though it belonged to a different era, long since passed. Yet that was impossible; she had just returned. She was certain she hadn't left anything behind. Doubt crept swiftly, insidiously undermining her certainty. Alice closed her eyes, focusing hard on her memory. The last clear recollection was stepping through the fracture, feeling the overwhelming sensation of merging with her lost self, reality mending around her. She had believed it was complete, seamless, but what if it wasn't?

Her eyes flicked open again, anxiety pushing her into motion. She reached urgently for her notebook, flipping through the pages with frantic precision. Everything seemed as it had been, the sketches, timelines, Harper Ross's cryptic messages. Yet, as she turned to the final page, her heart clenched painfully. The familiar words stared back at her: *Find the last.* But now beneath them, newly etched in ink that seemed impossibly fresh, were words she knew she had not written.

I'm still waiting.

Her breath slowed, the cold weight of dread settling deeply into her bones. Someone else had written those words. Someone she'd left behind.

Alice stood rigidly, thoughts racing in silent turmoil. The answer felt clear yet unbearable: Langley. Frederick Langley, who had guided her, whose fading image had haunted her since she returned. She'd assumed him gone, lost forever in the between-space of forgotten things. But what if he lingered still, trapped, suspended in a place beyond reach? Her fingers tightened around the note, crumpling it slightly. Guilt thickened in her chest, a slow, choking weight. She had left him there, alone, and now, through some impossible means, he was calling her back.

She stood motionless, breathing deeply, allowing the stark reality to settle fully around her. The choice was painfully simple: pretend the past was sealed, slip quietly back into the ordinary, or confront what she'd left unresolved.

Alice stared again at the fragile scrap of paper, its ink fading as though it didn't fully belong in this world. Perhaps it didn't. Perhaps neither did she. With decisive urgency, Alice exhaled, grabbed her coat, and stepped into the pale, uncertain dawn.

Chapter 44

Alice stepped into the early morning chill, the note crumpled tightly in her fist, the edges pressing into her palm. She didn't pack anything. She didn't write a note. Some part of her already knew where the path ended. Blackpool lay quiet before her, streets damp with mist and silence thick enough to feel oppressive, as though the entire town was holding its breath. It might have seemed peaceful, normal even to anyone else, but Alice knew better. She had seen beneath the ordinary façade, glimpsed too deeply into a fracture she wished she hadn't.

Turning the paper over slowly, she searched for any hidden meaning, but only the same three words were scrawled in her hesitant hand: *You left something.* Beneath that, another message had appeared, darker, almost accusatory.

I'm still waiting.

Alice exhaled sharply, anxiety tightening her chest, her destination unmistakably clear: the Winter Gardens, where reality had first fractured, where she'd nearly lost Langley and almost herself. Slipping the note into her coat pocket, she began walking, each step heavier than the last, dread settling in her with the morning chill.

When she reached the Winter Gardens, the thinning fog revealed the ornate façade in stark clarity, the morning light slicing coldly across carved stones and the iron gates beneath the vast, glass dome reflecting the dreary sky.

To anyone else, it might seem unchanged, trapped perpetually in the promise of another ordinary day, but Alice felt its strangeness as an ache deep in her bones.

Something had lingered here since the fire of 1895, a hidden remnant awaiting her return. Breathing air tainted by salt and rust, she pushed open the heavy doors.

Inside, emptiness swallowed her whole. Her footsteps echoed sharply off marble floors as she passed through the lobby toward the theatre entrance. A corridor stretched away from her into darkness. A corridor she was certain had never existed before. Yet it waited patiently, undeniably real, pulling at her curiosity as strongly as it repelled her reason. After only the briefest hesitation, Alice stepped forward, feeling the air grow colder, laced with the faint smell of damp rot. Shadows flickered from wall sconces, illuminating wallpaper peeling away in slow, forgotten decay. Whispers moved restlessly at the edge of hearing, murmuring unintelligible secrets.

Alice's breath quickened as she approached a pair of charred doors, edges blackened from a forgotten fire, the metal handle cold and rough beneath her fingers as she pushed, heart hammering fiercely. Beyond the doors, the theatre stretched endlessly into gloom, rows upon rows of empty seats facing a silent, dust-heavy stage. Each step creaked under her weight, the sound loud in the stillness, and as her eyes adjusted to the dimness, she saw him standing motionless at the stage's centre: Frederick Langley, illuminated by a pale, ghostly light.

"Langley," she breathed, her voice fragile in the vast emptiness.

He raised his head slowly, gaze hollow yet resigned, acknowledging her at last. "You finally came back."

Alice approached cautiously, heart racing. "You sent the note."

He inclined his head slightly, eyes weary but knowing. "Who else?"

Her voice faltered, barely audible. "I thought you were gone."

A faint smile touched his lips. "So did I."

Alice shivered; his voice felt displaced, drifting across layers of time and memory. "What happened?" she asked quietly, dreading the answer.

"You happened," he said softly, sadly. "I helped you escape, but I stayed behind."

Her throat tightened painfully; she had watched him fade, seen him vanish in smoke and flame, assuming the fracture had erased him entirely. But now he stood trapped within its cracks, impossibly present.

"We can fix it," she insisted, desperate to reclaim something of what was lost. "I escaped. I can bring you back with me."

Langley's expression didn't change, his weariness profound. Gently, quietly, he said the words she wasn't prepared to hear: "What if I don't want to leave?"

Alice froze, hands trembling slightly. "You don't belong here," she protested weakly.

Langley glanced around the theatre's infinite silence, his voice gentle but certain. "Maybe once I thought that. Maybe that's why I wrote the notes. Now, I'm not so sure. Here, reality doesn't shift or erase. Time doesn't move the same way. Here, things remain."

Her voice broke with urgency. "This is a fracture, a mistake. It isn't meant to exist."

"Yet here I am," he replied firmly, gently final.

She felt the fracture tightening around her, pulling subtly yet insistently. "If you don't leave now, you'll never leave," she pleaded, voice cracking.

Langley met her gaze, his resignation gentle yet unwavering. "Maybe that's how it's meant to be," he whispered softly.

Her vision blurred, sharp grief flooding through her, memories of Langley's hand gripping hers, smoke burning sharply in her lungs, his voice urging her from the flames, clear and comforting. She wanted desperately to argue, to fight for him, but understood with painful clarity that some choices weren't hers to make. With a heart grown unbearably heavy, Alice slowly turned away, the soft sound of doors closing behind her marking her return to a world now emptier than before.

Chapter 45

Alice stepped out of the Winter Gardens, the ornate façade behind her cast in shadows, its intricate details faded beneath the pale wash of dawn. The heavy doors closed slowly, their echo fading into the empty street like a forgotten melody. She stood caught momentarily between leaving and staying, the early morning chill biting sharply against her skin. Taking a deep breath, she steadied the trembling in her fingers and moved forward, her steps decisive yet burdened.

She had left Langley behind, and a complicated ache twisted within her, woven with choices made and opportunities lost. It had been his choice, as leaving was hers. Still, a faint, persistent regret pulled at the edge of her resolve, whispering gently what might have been. She tightened her fists, nails pressing painfully into her palms. If she allowed herself to glance back, she feared the unresolved yearning might overwhelm her, anchoring her forever to the spot.

The streets of Blackpool spread out before her in silence, bathed in a tentative dawn glow. Alice moved deliberately, retracing familiar routes that drew her into the heart of town: the comforting solidity of The Seagull's Rest, the austere reality of the Chronicle's office. Everything appeared intact, firm, and unyielding, free of distortions or vanished streets that had haunted her for weeks. Reality seemed finally restored, the rupture healed.

She exhaled slowly, relief tempered by profound weariness. For the first time in what felt like forever, Alice no longer needed to struggle to maintain her place within reality; it had finally consented to embrace her.

She felt whole yet irrevocably altered, carrying within her the unspoken scars of her journey.

The promenade stretched ahead, the distant cries of gulls blending into the soft murmurs of the sea. Pausing at the end of North Pier, Alice grasped the cold, weathered railing, the metal rough beneath her touch. The relentless wind brought the briny scent of salt and decay, tangling through her hair and tugging insistently at fragments of her memory. She had stood here before, her thoughts frayed and slipping toward dissolution. Now, only one Alice remained.

Her fingers brushed the crumpled note deep in her pocket. You left something, Langley had said. Himself, perhaps, or perhaps something more intangible, a piece of the woman who had battled fiercely to endure through those fragile, dissolving days. She was different now; the effortless trust she once held was shadowed by vigilance, scarred by a heightened sensitivity to the subtle tremors beneath reality's surface. Victorious but irrevocably changed, she knew no one in Blackpool would ever grasp the depths of what she had endured.

Alice took her notebook from her pocket, carefully turning to its final page. The messages had guided her through the darkness, cryptic warnings, haunting riddles. Her eyes fell upon the newest words, faintly inscribed by an unseen hand, words she knew she had never written.

Some doors never close.

The chill those words invoked was sharper than the cold morning wind, carrying a truth she was not yet ready to accept. She snapped the notebook shut, holding it suspended briefly over the railing, symbolising all the uncertainty she could never fully erase. Then, releasing her grip, she watched it vanish silently beneath the waves, swallowed whole by the restless tide, carrying away echoes of promises left unfulfilled.

Straightening her shoulders, Alice turned slowly away. With resolve and without hesitation, she began to walk, refusing to look back. Behind her, a solitary streetlamp flickered against the brightening sky, its glow sputtering like something refusing to die.

About the Author

Drawn irresistibly to hidden histories and tales better left forgotten, I explore characters who find themselves quietly stranded somewhere between comfort and creeping dread.

When not stuck in the realities of the day job, I usually roam aimlessly along the coast or lurk suspiciously in the neglected corners of historic towns, searching for stories stubborn enough to haunt the living.

Fractured Echoes is the first in a series of unsettling novels set in Blackpool. A town where nostalgia is treacherous, and reality is open to negotiation.

You can follow my adventures in researching random things on Twitter (X) @jeremynoad if I remember to post something.

Acknowledgements

If you're reading this, thank you. If you've bought the book as well, double thank you.

This is the part where I thank several people, most of whom you probably don't know and may never meet, but who were invaluable in bringing this book to life.

A heartfelt thank you to Dan Hanks for his guidance, patience, and skill in shaping the editing. Gratitude also to Nick Castle (www.nickcastledesign.com) for creating a perfect cover that captures the essence of the story.

Thanks to Grammarly, without whose support on commas, full stops, and sentence structure, this could easily have become a single, very long sentence disguised as a story.

To my family, Helen, Elliott, and Megan, thank you for your endless patience and for never questioning my repeated claims of 'working.' (I suspect you thought I was simply putting in overtime.)

Finally, immense gratitude to Aimée, Carrie, Gabby, Victoria, Mary, Louise, Caroline, and Harry. Your thoughtful insights and feedback during the drafting stages were invaluable and deeply appreciated.

Thank you all.